BRITTA'S JOURNEY

AN EMIGRATION SAGA

BRITTA'S JOURNEY
AN EMIGRATION SAGA

Ann Marie Mershon

Illustrations by
Gail Alden-Hedstrom

Singing River Publications, Inc.
2004

BRITTA'S JOURNEY: an emigration saga
by Ann Marie Mershon

Illustrations by:
Gail Alden-Hedstrom

Final Edit, Layout and Production by:
Charles Morello
IRIS Enterprises
Eveleth, MN 55734

Published by:

Singing River Publications, Inc.
P.O. Box 72
Ely, MN 55731-0072
www.singingriverpublications.com

Printed in Canada by
Friesens Corporation
Altona, Manitoba

ISBN: 0-9709575-6-4

1. Emigration; 2. Children's Story; 3. Inspiration;

In memory of
Eleanor Jacobson Stone,
whose compelling story
and bright spirit live on
in the character of Britta

INTRODUCTION

In the early 1900's, many Scandinavians moved to Minnesota. They were willing to sacrifice much and suffer many hardships to start a new life in America. Britta's Journey is based on the actual emigration experience of the Jacobsons, a Swedish-speaking family from Kvevlax, Finland. After losing three children to illness in Finland, Johan Erik and Maria Jacobson decided to leave poverty behind and emigrate to America. Johan Erik traveled alone to Minnesota in 1900, hoping to send for the rest of his family within a year. They never imagined it would be over four years before they saw each other again.

Contents

BRITTA'S JOURNEY
AN EMIGRATION SAGA

CHAPTER 1
THE TRAIN TO HANGO
1904

Britta woke confused. What was that thrumming sound? She rubbed her eyes and looked up. The train! Oh yes– she was on her way to America. To Papa! Outside her window the sun sat low in the sky. She must have slept for hours. Pipe smoke hung in a haze over the passengers. It reminded her of Papa– a warm, cozy smell. It wouldn't be long now! Her stomach fluttered. What if they never got there? What if Papa couldn't find them? America was a big place, wasn't it?

Elsa was sound asleep, curled up beside Britta with her hair sweaty against the brown leather seat. Arvid's head hung over into the aisle, his mouth gaping and his blonde curls dangling. Even Mama nodded over the knitting in her lap.

Britta reached into her bag to pet Lisel. Her kitten. Her secret. She had to keep her hidden until they got on the ship, then it would be too late for Mama to say no. She

hoped the ship would be waiting near the train station, otherwise how would they ever find their way? If only Papa were here to guide them. Of course, there was Johan– the Man of the Family. Humph. With him in charge, they'd never get there.

She looked over to see if Johan was asleep, too, but his seat was empty. Gone again! That Johan was always disappearing. And he was the oldest. Some brother! Sometimes Britta got sick of looking out for him. He should be looking out for her.

Britta's throat tightened as she remembered how Johan had disappeared earlier that morning. They had been ready to leave for the train station, and Mama had sent her to find him– as usual! She'd raced across the barnyard after him, long, blonde braids flying behind her.

"Johan! Where ARE you?" she'd called. It was just like him to make them late– to make them miss the train. She'd find him, though– maybe up in the woods.

Britta was breathless by the time she reached the trees. Sweat stung her eyes and loose hairs clung to her neck. She paused to wipe her forehead and survey the woods, dense with birch trees and thimbleberry bushes. The dark woods were filled with bears and wolves. How would she ever find Johan?

"Johan! You'd better come out– right now!" she called, hardly recognizing her own shrill voice. She glanced back at the house, at Uncle Jacob loading the trunks into the wagon. Her heart raced. What if he was hiding? Was he afraid to go to America?

She hesitated, gulped, and took a deep breath. Bears or no bears, she had to find her brother.

"Johan! Come out right this minute!" she screamed. He was some Man of the Family– thirteen years old, and still he acted like a rascal. They had to leave for Vaasa right away! What was wrong with him?

She swallowed her fear and ran into the

woods, calling, "Johan! Johan!" If he was hurt, could she carry him? He might be lost– maybe forever! That couldn't be– he knew the woods too well. But Britta could get lost– or attacked by a wolf or a bear. She might be killed! Uncle Jacob would come up to the woods and find her clothes and bits of her spread everywhere.

Britta ran frantically, searching the trees for any sign of her brother.

"Johan!" She called, then stopped. Was that a growl? She wheeled around and froze. Where had it come from? She needed a stick to defend herself. Her heart pounded nearly out of her chest. Calm down, Britta thought. Calm down. There's no bear.

Suddenly, something heavy dropped onto her back, and she crumbled beneath it. She shrieked and scrambled to escape, then remembered what Papa had told her about bears. She squeezed her eyes shut and rolled into a ball. If she played dead, the bear would leave her alone. "Please, God" she prayed as she lay still as a stone.

Time stopped. The woods were silent. Slowly, Britta opened her eyes.

Johan stood above her, grinning mischievously. She jumped to her feet, blue eyes blazing.

"You're horrible, Johan! I hate you!" she shrieked as she lunged at him, arms flailing. Her fury exploded as she pounded his chest.

Britta blushed as she remembered. Johan always brought out the worst in her. Well, she'd found him, and they were finally on their way– to Papa and to America!

A sharp stab pulled her back to reality. Lisel! She pulled a tiny orange kitten out of her cloth bag and examined her bleeding finger. "You little stinker!" she whispered, tapping the kitten on her nose. Then she held it to her cheek as she clambered past the sleeping twins to hunt for Johan.

The car was quiet. People slept or watched the scenery roll past their windows, many curled up under coats and jackets. A few talked in hushed whispers. Britta scanned each seat she passed. Had Johan found a new friend? Her eyes narrowed as she thought of his school friend, Halmar. Why was it so easy for Johan to make friends?

There was no sign of Johan anywhere. Britta pulled at the heavy door to the next car, then stopped short, petrified. There was a narrow platform outside the door, and a two-foot gap before the next platform– over moving track! The ground was a blur beneath her. Britta closed the door and leaned back against it, her heart in her throat. She could never make that jump to the next car. Not with the train moving!

"Who cares about stupid Johan anyway?" she thought. "If he's lost, he can just stay lost. He never worries about me."

As she started back to her seat, she thought of how Johan always made fun of her for being a coward. She remembered, too, how Mama was always proud of Johan for being brave– "my brave little soldier" Mama called him. Well, Britta could be brave, too. She could do anything Johan could do, and she'd prove it!

She marched back to the end of the train car, opened the door again, took a deep breath, and stepped out onto the platform. The wind whooshed up under her skirt, blowing it into her face. As she pushed it down, the gravel roadbed popped into view, whizzing by at top speed beneath her. What if she slipped? She'd be crushed! She could die! She'd hardly noticed the long step when they were hunting for seats, but now that the train was moving, it terrified her. She wanted to turn back, but what would that prove? Johan would just make fun of her again.

"Please, God, keep me safe!" she prayed, then took another look at the track below. If Johan had done it, she could too.

"Don't look down. Don't look down," Britta told herself. "Get ready, Kitty. We're going to jump." She slipped the kitten into her apron pocket and clutched the long metal bar beside the door. She took a deep breath, reached her other hand toward the next car's metal bar, counted to three, and and leaped across to the next platform. She felt her boot hit the platform, but when she looked down, she lost her balance. Her foot slipped off the platform.

"Help!" she screamed as she grabbed frantically for the bar beside the door. Her fingers closed around it, and she clung desperately. Her heart pounded in her throat as she hauled herself back up onto the platform. She stood frozen until her heart settled. As she took a deep breath, a slow smile spread across her face.

The kitten mewed, clawing its way up out of her pocket. Britta closed her hand around its tiny neck and lifted it to her cheek. "We made it, Lisel. We made it!" She looked up into the sky and said, "Thank you, God."

Britta's blue eyes sparkled as she stepped through the door into the next car. She had done it! She couldn't wait to tell Papa.

CHAPTER 2
HUNTING FOR JOHAN

Britta searched through the next car for Johan. She heard a language that sounded more rough and throaty than Swedish. Was it Finnish? Swedish sounded so much more friendly; she was glad to be a Swede-Finn. Johan wasn't in that car, so she went on, hesitating before she opened the door to the next platform.

Once on the platform, she stood frozen with her back against the door for a few long minutes before she could force herself to jump. This time she wouldn't look down. She focused on the opposite platform, took a deep breath and jumped. She grabbed at the handrail beside the door and let out a huge, relieved sigh. Her hand shook as she lifted Lisel from her pocket, and when the kitten squealed, she loosened her grip.

"I'm sorry, Lisel. I didn't mean to squeeze you," she crooned as she cradled the kitten next to her cheek.

Johan wasn't in the next car either.

Where could he be? Had he gone in the other direction? She checked two more cars, carefully scanning every face.

As she stood at the end of the last car, a gray-haired woman near the aisle tapped her elbow and asked in Swedish, "Are you looking for someone, *Flicka*?" Though the woman's clouded eyes were buried in folds of wrinkles, her warm smile put Britta at ease. "Yes, ma'am. I'm looking for my brother. He has straight white hair, blue eyes, and lots of freckles. Have you seen him?"

The old woman chuckled as she tapped claw-like fingers on the arm of her seat. "I'm afraid most of the boys on the train fit that description, my dear. But no boys have come into this car in the last hour or so. I have nothing to do but watch, you know."

"Thank you," Britta said, and with a nod, she was off to retrace her steps. On the way back, she made a game of jumping between cars. She pretended she was an acrobat leaping from her trapeze to a high platform. People applauded wildly as she completed each jump, so she took a quick bow and held Lisel up to the excited crowd before opening the door into the next car. She even made her last jump holding Lisel in one hand. A man opened the door just as she was taking her bow. She bent her head low and hurried on, cheeks burning.

When she returned to her seat, she

found Johan watching the rugged coast of the Baltic stream by the window– her window. She hid Lisel behind her back.

"Where were you?" she hissed across Elsa's curled up body.

"Where were you?" Johan mimicked.

"You took my seat!" Britta said, sticking out her tongue as she settled onto the bench and slipped Lisel into her pocket.

"Well, I'm the Man of the Family, so I'll sit where I like. And what are you hiding?"

"Nothing," Britta answered, revealing her empty hands. Johan craned his neck to look behind her.

Britta's throat tightened. She didn't need Johan snooping into her business. She thought quickly.

"Are you hungry?" she asked as she knelt to rummage through Mama's big home-spun bag. She found a few hard rye rolls and handed one to Johan. The dark molasses and rye tasted like home. Britta felt a lump in her throat as she thought of Vistaso with its huge boulders, its barn loft, and its kitchen garden. She remembered how the round rye loaves were hung from the rafters in the kitchen. Would they have rafters in America? Would she ever see home again? She shook the thought from her mind. She didn't care. She wanted to be with Papa, and wherever Papa was would be home. She slipped a bit of roll into her pocket for Lisel.

"Look at the sky, Johan. It's turning lavender and pink."

Johan nodded as he chewed his bread. He didn't even look up.

"I wonder how far it is to Hango," Britta said.

"We'll be there before dark."

Britta bristled. What a know-it-all he was. "And how do you know?"

"I asked, bird brain. A man in a uniform said we'd be there by dark. He said we'll spend the night in a hotel."

"A hotel! I'm sure we can't afford that!" Britta gasped.

"Well, don't believe it then. Suit yourself."

Britta knew better than to argue with The Man of the Family. "We'll see," she said.

She marveled as the sun performed its evening magic on the clouds. The countryside looked just like home, mostly fields dotted with huge boulders. How she loved climbing those huge rocks! She remembered how Papa hid behind them and jumped out to tickle her until she cried for mercy. Would there be boulders in America? Or birch trees or great white pines? Britta wondered if she'd miss Finland. America was sure to be better! They'd be rich and live in a big house with a pantry full of food. And they'd be with Papa! A shiver of delight tingled her spine.

Before long Elsa stretched herself

awake, and Arvid popped to his feet. Finally Mama opened her eyes, too. While Mama was occupied with the twins, Britta slipped her kitten into the cloth bag and stashed it under her seat where no one would notice if it wiggled. She knew the clatter of the train on the tracks would cover any mewing.

"Look, Mama! Houses!" Elsa said, pointing out the window. There were more and more houses, all red with white trim. Every house had a garden, some with purple lupine and others with bright orange poppies.

"Yes, Elsa. We must be getting to Hango," Mama answered.

Arvid wriggled in his seat. "I need the outhouse," he announced.

"It's not an outhouse, it's a room on the train," Johan said with authority. "It's the W.C., and I know where it is. I'll show you."

"Bring the girls, too," Mama suggested. "I'll put together a little supper while you're gone."

Britta took Elsa's and Arvid's hands and followed Johan toward the front of the car. "Wait," she called. "The twins will need help getting across between the cars. You go first, and I'll hand them to you."

"You'll need some help, too, scaredy-skirts," Johan taunted in a soft voice that only Britta could hear.

She shot him a tight-lipped glare. She'd show him!

Johan waited to lift Elsa and Arvid across, but when he reached a hand to Britta, she shook her head and leapt nimbly to the next platform. Johan didn't say a word, but Britta knew he was surprised.

Elsa and Arvid stared wide-eyed into the water closet. They had never seen an indoor toilet. A tiny room held a wooden box with a seat on it, much like the outhouse at home, only nicer, with a rounded wood seat and brass trim.

"Girls first," Britta said, closing the door on the boys. When she lifted the lid, there was a loud whoosh of noise and air. The hole led straight to the outside! Britta could see gravel whizzing by under the train. She needed to relieve herself, though, so she lifted her skirts and did it as quickly as she could.

"Now you, Elsa," Britta said.

Elsa balked. "I don't want to."

"But you should go now while we're here, Elsa."

"I might fall in!" Elsa said, tears welling in her eyes.

"I'll hold you."

"No! I won't. I won't, I won't, I won't!" Elsa stormed.

"All right. I won't make you." Britta tousled her curls and smiled to herself. Elsa had a mind of her own, and there was never any changing it. "You little goose. You'll just have to hold it then."

When they got back to their seats, Mama had put out a picnic of hard rolls, cheese, and a sliced apple. "Fill your bellies, children. We have to eat well to stay healthy for the long trip."

"How long will it take, Mama?" Arvid asked.

"I think a few weeks," she answered, "but I don't know. I wish your papa were with us. I'm afraid it may be a hard trip. Of course, we have Johan."

Britta rolled her eyes. The Man of the Family. Good old reliable Johan.

They munched their dinner as they watched the countryside grow more and more populated under the darkening sky.

"Next stop, Hango," a man in a dark blue uniform announced as he walked down the aisle. "Five minutes." Then he repeated it in the other language Britta had heard.

"Was that Finnish, Mama?" she asked. "I imagine so. Gather your things, children. Britta, you hold onto Elsa, and Johan, you hold onto Arvid. I'll carry your bags."

"I'll carry mine," Britta said as she swept her bag from under the seat and set it gently into her lap.

A shrill whistle filled the air, and the train slowed to a crawl as it entered Hango. Brick buildings were tinted with lavender in the twilight. Britta felt a tug at her sleeve.

"Britta," Elsa whispered into her ear, "I

wet myself."

"Oh, Elsa!" Britta sighed and shook her head. "Why didn't you go when I told you?" She pulled Elsa's sopping dress out from beneath her. "Well, there's nothing to be done now. You'll just have to wait until we get to the hotel."

Elsa's eyes brimmed with tears.

Britta bent to Elsa and whispered, "Then I'll show you a surprise I have in my bag. It will be our very own secret." She patted her bag gently and gave Elsa a reassuring hug.

CHAPTER 3
HANGO HOTEL

Dark had settled on Hango by the time they got off the train. A sea breeze blew on the backs of the travelers as they trudged across the street to the hotel. The strange ocean scent and the distant lapping of waves filled Britta's senses. Heavy smells reached to her through the darkness. She wondered if their ship stood waiting for them on a nearby pier. How she wished she could see it!

"Aren't we going to get our trunks, Mama?" Britta asked.

"Everyone else is going to the hotel, Britta, and we'll do what they do."

"But we need our quilts, and Elsa needs dry clothes." Britta heard her voice break into that childish whine she hated so much, but she couldn't help it. She wished Mama would ask someone. If Papa were there, he would have found out what was happening.

"Britta! That's enough! We're going with everyone else. They'll have beds in the hotel, and I have extra things for Elsa."

"I'm tired!" Arvid complained.

"Me, too," whimpered Elsa.

"Enough! Everyone's tired, and we'll have a bed soon. Now come along!" Mama ordered. She grasped Elsa and Arvid's hands and marched over to join the long line of weary travelers outside the hotel.

The two-story brick building was longer than four farmhouses, and warm light glowed through every window. Britta wondered which room would be theirs. She couldn't wait to collapse into bed. Maybe there would even be a fluffy eiderdown quilt! She smiled to herself as she imagined an elegant room waiting for them upstairs. It would have a carved wooden bed and a washstand and a brightly-painted rocker. Why was the line so slow? It felt like hours before they reached the entrance to the hotel.

Britta stared wide-eyed into the vast lobby. What a madhouse it was! The orderly line outside had turned to chaos inside. People were crowded like sardines in the most beautiful room Britta had ever seen. The walls were covered with patterned wallpaper, and the doors and windows were decorated in bright rosmaling with golden accents that glittered in the flickering gaslight. She had never seen anything so lovely. This is what America will be, she thought with a smile. Even the streets there are lined with gold.

Mama murmured, "Oh, my goodness. How I wish your papa was here! What do we do?"

"I'll go see," Britta offered.

"No, me! I'm the oldest, and the MAN of the Family," Johan announced, shoving Britta aside. Britta shoved him right back, then gave him a kick in the shin for good measure.

"Stop that!" Mama scolded. "Johan, you go find out what's going on. We'll wait right here. Britta, you will act like a young lady." Britta seethed as Johan strutted importantly across the room.

Britta saw Johan marching back, all puffed up and important like a big toad. "There are no more rooms. Our ticket includes a room, but they're all full," he said. "Lots of people are angry, but the man said there's nothing to be done. They have blankets for us so we can sleep on the floor. They'll have breakfast for us tomorrow, then we can board the ship."

"Oh, dear. We have to sleep on this hard wooden floor?" Mama said, looking around for an open space to settle.

"I'll find a spot for us," Johan said, heading back toward the crowd.

Britta spotted an open rug near the doorway. "Here, Mama! Here's a soft spot!" Johan turned at her voice, and she wrinkled her nose at him, careful not to let Mama see.

"It will have to do," said Mama. "Johan, you go get blankets. Britta, you get Elsa into some dry clothes," she said, stroking Elsa's hair. "Poor thing."

Britta set her chin angrily as she dug through Mama's bag. Johan always got to do the fun jobs. Always! She found a dry dress and under-linens, then turned her back to the room and hurried Elsa out of her wet clothes and into dry ones. "You're too big to be wetting yourself!" she scolded. Elsa hung her head.

Britta felt an immediate stab of guilt. How could she be so hard on Elsa, her little pumpkin? She didn't mean to be cruel. Elsa couldn't help it. Then she remembered her promise. She lifted Elsa onto her lap and opened her cloth bag just wide enough for Elsa to peek inside.

"Shhh, now. This is our little secret, Elsa. Not a word to anyone!"

Elsa grinned up at Britta, eyes sparkling. "It's Lisel!" she whispered and reached in to touch the kitten– the rust-colored kitten that was their favorite of the new litter.

Britta held a finger to her mouth. "Not a word, remember, or Mama will make us leave her behind!" Elsa threw her arms around Britta's neck and clung to her, then kissed her right on the mouth.

"Time for bed, girls," Mama said.

"Yes, Mama," they chorused as Britta slipped another scrap of bread to the kitten. She and Elsa curled together with the mewing bag between them. Britta smiled. With all the whining and chatter in the room, Mama would never hear it.

The next morning, Britta awoke to a buzz of whispers. Where was she? She rubbed her eyes. Oh, yes. The hotel! Early morning sun slanted through the windows on clusters of sleeping bodies. Some were curled under blankets, while others slept sitting up against the walls.

She loosened the bag from Elsa's grasp, then reached inside for the kitten. It was gone! Had Elsa taken her out? Did Lisel work the laces open? Britta lifted Elsa's blanket. No kitten.

Britta scrambled up to look for Lisel. She was so tiny– she could be anywhere! Mama was still asleep with Arvid snuggled beside her. Thank goodness the kitten wasn't climbing on Mama! Britta noticed a red-head-ed girl about her age watching her from a spot on the other side of the door. Britta nodded and smiled. The girl's face widened into a gap-toothed grin.

Britta stepped carefully over Elsa and scanned the room for a wiggling orange fur ball. The red-headed girl hopped up to follow her. "What are you doing?" she whispered.

"I've lost my kitten, and I have to find her before Mama wakes up!"

"I saw a little orange kitten follow someone outside," the girl offered.

"Oh, thank you!" Britta said, heading for the door.

The red-headed girl joined her. "My name is Hilda," she said once they were outside.

"I'm Britta," she answered, peering around a bush.

"I'll help you look for your kitten. What's its name? Is it a boy or a girl? Where did you get it? Are you taking it on the boat?"

"Her name is Lisel," Britta said, bending to look under some lilacs. "Our cat had kittens just before we left, and Lisel was my favorite, so I brought her along at the last minute. I was afraid Mama would make me leave her behind, so I didn't tell her," she continued as they walked down the gravel path, searching the yard. "I have to keep her hidden until she's safely on the ship– if I ever find her!" She hurried around the corner of the building, her eyes darting everywhere a kitten might go. She was losing hope.

"We'll find her. She just went out a minute ago," Hilda said confidently. "Maybe we'll be on the same ship to England."

"We're going to America– not England. Papa is waiting for us. I haven't seen him in four years, and I really miss him." She peeked behind a pile of firewood.

"You haven't seen your papa in four years? That's awful! How can you stand it? Don't you know that all the ships from here go to England? We have to change there to a big ocean steamship for America."

"Oh, no! That's terrible! I'll never be able keep my kitten a secret that long." Britta lifted huge hosta leaves to peer under them.

"I can help you," Hilda assured her. "We can do it together if we're on the same ship."

"Where are you going?"

"We're going to America to be with my auntie and uncle who moved to Minnesota," Hilda said as she peeked behind a juniper bush.

"I'm going to Minnesota, too! Maybe we'll be neighbors!" Britta exclaimed. She headed for a rhubarb plant in the corner of the yard– a likely hiding place for a mischievous kitten.

"Would you like to be my friend?" Hilda asked.

Britta stopped hunting for a moment. "Oh, yes! I'd like that. I've never had a friend my age. It's mostly boys at my school, and they never let me join their games." Most people in Kvevlax thought school was a waste of time for girls, so Britta had spent many hours sitting alone with her lunch.

"Look! There she is, heading for that puddle!" Hilda exclaimed.

Britta ran to scoop the tiny kitten into her arms. "Lisel! You scared me. I thought I'd never see you again. Shame on you!"

"Can I hold her?" Hilda asked.

Britta nestled the mewing kitten into Hilda's pudgy, outstretched hands. As Hilda cuddled it to her cheek, Britta noticed that she had so many freckles some of them ran together.

"I bet she's thirsty," Hilda announced. She set Lisel down gently at the edge of the puddle, where she lapped eagerly at the muddy water.

"I guess she was!" Britta smiled, finally picking her up to cuddle against her own paler cheek. "I'm thirsty too, but I wouldn't drink that dirty water!"

"No– ish!" they said at the very same moment. They giggled, then turned to go back inside. Britta gave Lisel a little kiss on the nose and slid her into the pocket of her apron. Lisel scrabbled up the fabric out of the pocket, and Britta laughed as she pushed her back down. "You have to stay hidden until we get on the ship, Lisel!"

The lobby had come to life. Children yawned and stretched as adults folded blankets and packed up their belongings. "I'll see you later, Britta," Hilda called as she skipped off to join her parents. A table had been set up with food for the travelers, and an orderly line had formed. Britta spotted Johan in the line, so she joined Mama and the little ones.

"Where were you?" Mama asked.

"I was outside with my new friend," Britta beamed.

"So you've made a friend," Mama said. "But right now there's work to be done. Help me fold these blankets, and then you can help Johan carry the food."

Britta bent over Elsa and slipped the kitten back into her bag. She handed it to Elsa with a wink. When Elsa cradled it in her arms like a baby, Britta cringed, hoping Mama wouldn't notice. They finished folding the blankets, and after a warning glance to Elsa, Britta scooted off to help Johan. He was at the front of the line, and she watched as he was given five thick slices of rye bread with cheese. He handed them to Britta, then picked up a pottery jug filled with fresh milk.

"It looks delicious, doesn't it?" Britta said as she handed out the warm rye bread. No one answered– they were busy stuffing their mouths, hungry as springtime bears.

Later that morning the emigrants were guided to the ship.

When they arrived at the wharf, Britta stared wide-eyed. There were boats every-where– bright blue and red fishing boats, sail-boats, and flatboats. They bobbed cheerfully in the swells and dips of the deep, dark water. How would they ever know which boat was theirs? Maybe it was written on the tickets.

"Mama! Mama! This way!" Johan called from far ahead, standing by the biggest boat on the pier.

It was longer than two hotels! Maybe three! The boat was painted white and had a huge smokestack slanting up from what looked like a house sitting on the middle of the deck. There were two tall masts, one on each end of the deck, and they flew the Finnish flag. Ropes as thick as Britta's arm held the ship to stout posts on the dock. Workers hustled up and down a wooden ramp lugging boxes and trunks of all sizes. *Arcturus* was painted on the back of the ship, and along each side, long rowboats hung from cables above the deck.

"What are those boats for? Britta asked.

Johan answered with a sly grin. "They're in case we sink!"

Britta's stomach lurched. In case we sink!

CHAPTER 4
THE BOAT TO HULL, ENGLAND

"Line up here for the ship to Hull, England! Families line up together behind the father!" ordered a stout, balding man, first in Finnish, then in Swedish.

People bustled to follow these directions in the midst of tooting tugboats and clattering wagons along the pier. Britta felt a pang of loneliness as she watched all the families of children line up behind their fathers.

Mama herded her children into the line. "Johan, you're the Man of the Family. You'll go first. I'll stand behind you with the twins. You go last, Britta, to make sure we don't lose the little ones." Johan wrinkled his nose at Britta as he pushed her aside and moved to the front of the family. Britta shot Johan a sideways glare, then took her place at the back.

Britta tried to focus on the twins, but she couldn't stop staring at the mammoth ship that would bring them to England. People trudged up a huge wooden ramp car-

rying rucksacks or pulling trunks behind
them. There had to be room for more than a
hundred people on the *Arcturus*. It was mon-
strous.

An officer questioned the father of a
large family, then sent them off to one side,
where they huddled together. Britta clutched
her bag tighter as she realized that they, too,
might be sent aside.

"Please, God, let us get on the boat!"
she prayed.

Johan and Mama finally stepped to the
front of the line.

"*Suomalainen? Svenska?* (Finnish?
Swedish?)" asked a ruddy-faced man.

"Swedish," Johan answered. "We're Swede-Finns."

"Have any of you been sick in the last month?"

"No."

"Any fevers in the past week?"

"No."

"Where will you settle in America?"

"In Minnesota."

"Is someone waiting for you there?"

"My father, Johan Erik Jacobson."

"Do you speak English?"

"No."

"Do you have extra food for your journey?"

Johan turned to Mama with a question in his eyes. "Thirty loaves of rye bread and five wheels of cheese," she said.

The man nodded. "How much money?"

"Thirty American dollars that my husband sent me."

"Hang on to it. You'll need it to enter the United States."

He looked each of them over carefully, then said, "Show me your tickets and passports, then."

Mama rummaged in her bag for the large, brown envelope that held their packet of papers. She handed it all to the officer, who recorded their names on a list, then returned the packet and said, "Pick up your trunks and board the ship."

Britta sighed with relief as they filed past him toward the luggage piled on the pier. She and Johan dragged one trunk while Mama strained to pull the other one up the long ramp. By the time they had hauled everything up on the deck, they were dripping with sweat. "Well, I guess we're on our way," Mama said, "and we managed without your Papa. Good work, Johan." Britta looked to her mother for praise, but there was none for her.

She peered back at the dock and spotted Hilda's red curls below them.

"Hilda!" she called. "Look up!"

Hilda waved. "Wait for me!"

"So that's your new friend," Mama said. "You'll have time for her later. Right now we need to find a place to settle ourselves for the trip. I heard someone say we won't reach England until late in the night, so we must find a place to sit before the spots are all taken. Come, children."

"Coming, Mama!" chorused Arvid and Elsa.

"Not me!" Johan said. "I want to explore!"

"First we find a seat, Johan. Then you can disappear," Mama said in her no-nonsense voice. "The Man of the Family takes care of his family first."

Britta grinned at Johan but said nothing.

They found a bench inside the building

with enough space for all five of them. Windows encircled the room. Britta noticed that the benches were bolted to the floor– bright red benches that made the room festive, just like she felt.

"Good-bye, Mama!" Johan said as he headed off.

"May I go find Hilda now, Mama?" Britta asked.

"You can if you promise to keep an eye on Johan for me," Mama answered.

"But, Mama! He's the oldest. Why do I always have to keep an eye on him? And how can I do it if I don't know where he went?" Britta put her hands on her hips. "It's not fair!"

"Well, life isn't fair, young lady. You know how Johan is always wandering off. You're the sensible one. If you want, I'll watch for him and you can stay here with Elsa and Arvid."

"I'll look for him," Britta mumbled. Maybe Hilda would help. She hoped Hilda didn't have brothers and sisters to watch out for, too.

WHOOT! WHOOT! The horn blasted through the air as the huge ship churned away from the dock. Britta and Hilda stood at the railing with the throng of passengers waving goodbye to their homeland.

Britta's eyes searched out the family

that had been left behind. They stood like statues behind the bustling and waving crowd as the ship headed out onto the Baltic Sea without them. She wondered why they had been turned away. At least it wasn't her. Her heart would break if she had to wait one more minute to be on her way to Papa.

She missed him so, and she knew he must be lonesome without them! Britta was sure Mama's old happy self would return once they were a family again. Mama never laughed anymore– at least not like she used to when Papa teased her and played music for them. Britta smiled as she remembered one day when Papa had plunked Mama in the wheelbarrow and run through the barnyard with Mama screeching and laughing. Those were such good times! It had been a long, lonely four years without Papa.

"Where's your kitten?" Hilda asked. "Can I hold her?"

"Here she is," Britta said, lifting the sleepy kitten tenderly from her sack. She gave it a quick kiss on the nose before handing it to Hilda. "Be careful not to drop her into the water."

"Oh, don't be silly, Britta. How could I? Oh, Kitty, you're so sweeeeet!" Hilda cooed. She rubbed the kitten against her cheek. "And so soft! Do you think she's thirsty? She seems tired or hungry or something."

Hilda sure fussed a lot over Lisel. You'd

think she'd never seen a kitten. Britta reached to take Lisel back, then checked herself. She didn't want to lose her new friend over a kitten.

The boat began to rock. Britta gazed out ahead, astonished at the huge swells on the ocean. These weren't just waves– they were hills of water with sun glinting across their crests.

"Hilda! Look at the sparkling waves. It's like magic!" Britta knew she should be hunting for Johan, but Hilda was more fun.

"And look back, Britta. This may be our last sight of Finland for ever and ever and ever!" Hilda said. The girls stood in silence, watching the land grow smaller and smaller on the horizon.

Britta blinked back a tear. She refused to be sad about leaving Grandmama and Aunt Anna and Uncle Jacob. "Well, we might come back some day. We'll be rich in America, you know," she declared, reaching for the kitten. She braced her legs as the boat took a lurch, and her stomach did a somersault.

Hilda held Lisel up toward the sky and grinned at Britta.

"Oh, you are soooo sweet!" she cooed, stroking the kitten's nose. She turned back to Britta. "Has your mama noticed yet?"

"I don't think so. I'm not sure how long I can keep her secret, though. She doesn't like being cooped up. She's always trying to scramble out of her sack." Britta reached for the railing and waited for her stomach to settle.

"How about if I pretend she's mine? I'll keep her half the time, and we'll tell your mama that she's mine. Then we can tell my mama that she's yours. How about that?" Hilda suggested.

Britta hesitated. But then, wasn't sharing Lisel better than keeping her hidden in a sack or a pocket all the time? "I guess so. Let me explain it to my little sister Elsa first. She's the only one who knows. Then I'll tell Mama."

Britta scanned the deck. "Will you help me look for my brother? Mama said I had to keep an eye on him."

"I saw some boys climbing a ladder to the upper deck."

"I'll bet it was Johan. Show me where."

Britta followed Hilda along the deck to the ladder, wobbling and weaving as the ship heaved back and forth on the waves. Britta felt dizzy, but she took a deep breath and kept moving.

"I'll take Lisel now," she said. "I better put her in my pocket."

"Here's where they went up," Hilda announced, grabbing the ladder to keep her balance on the pitching deck. She lifted her skirt and held it to one side with her left hand as she started to climb. She held the ladder with her right hand, sliding it along as she worked her way up, one rung at a time. Suddenly, the boat pitched violently, throwing her backward onto the deck.

Hilda's head made a cracking sound as she hit. She didn't move or say anything. Was she dead? Britta gasped and bent over her. Was she breathing? She held Hilda's cheeks and looked into her face. "Open your eyes, Hilda!" she cried. "Are you all right?"

Hilda's green eyes fluttered open and she looked up at Britta weakly. "I think I'm dying. Farewell!" She swept a hand dramatically across her forehead and pretended to faint– but not before Britta caught the playful glint in her green eyes.

"Oh, you scared me!" Britta said. Hilda's blank face transformed to a teasing grin, and they both burst into giggles.

"I really did bump my head, though, and it hurts." Hilda rubbed the back of her head as she sat up. "Maybe it's too wavy to climb a ladder, especially in a skirt!"

"Sometimes I hate being a girl," Britta said. "If you wore trousers, you'd have two hands for the ladder."

"Yes, but boys don't get to have pretty long hair, and you have to admit that dresses look nicer than trousers. Especially on girls!" Hilda giggled.

Hilda's dresses were pretty. Britta's

homespun dresses were boring, even if Mama did dye them bright colors.

Britta's stomach was starting to feel terrible. "Johan!" she called. "Johan? Are you up there?"

A mop of light hair framed in a halo of sunlight appeared over the upper railing. "Hey, Britta! Come on up! It's fun! The captain is showing us how to steer the ship!"

"No, thanks," Britta said. She would have loved to see the upper deck and the captain's room, but she wasn't going to risk the ladder.

The boat was rolling harder now, and Britta's stomach felt worse by the minute. She looked out over the water, hoping to regain her sense of balance.

"I think I need to go inside, Hilda."

But Hilda didn't answer. She was bent over the railing, vomiting into the water. Britta stood beside her, bent forward, and emptied her stomach into the Baltic Sea.

She clung to the railing, heaving until there was nothing left. Weak and trembling, she lowered herself to the deck, holding tight to the metal railing. Hilda had already collapsed, exhausted. The new friends sat together, gazing blankly across the rolling waves.

CHAPTER 5
SEASICK

Britta felt miserable. People were draped across benches and against the railing all along the deck. Would their whole trip be like this? Britta tried to close her eyes, but it only made things worse. She watched the tiny tip of the Hango lighthouse grow smaller on the horizon.

"Goodbye, Finland," she whispered.

When the beacon disappeared, Britta watched the lifeboats swinging above her for a while, but that just made her dizzier. She closed her eyes for a hasty prayer: "Please, God, bring us safely to England."

Britta felt sure the voyage would never end. She slouched against the wall for hours. She hardly noticed when Hilda left. The sounds of crashing waves and moaning passengers filled the air. Britta's throat stung from vomiting.

Finally, she mustered the strength to drag herself inside. Mama and the twins looked as green as Britta felt. The room reeked with the sharp stench of vomit, and people were scattered everywhere– stretched limply on the benches and curled up on the floor.

Britta sat beside Elsa and whispered, "I'm going to tell Mama that Lisel is Hilda's kitten. Then we can play with her. Don't tell!"

Elsa nodded weakly, her blue eyes vacant. Britta wasn't sure she'd even heard.

Britta reached into her pocket and pulled out the sleeping kitten. "Look, Mama. Hilda has a kitten, and I'm going to take care of it for a while. Hilda's too sick." Britta bit her lower lip. It was hard to lie.

Mama lifted her head. Her shoulders drooped, but she managed a smile. "She's just like one of the kittens we left at home. What's her name?"

"Lisel."

"Did you find Johan?" Mama asked.

Always Johan– Johan, Johan, Johan. Britta sighed. "He's up on the top deck with some other boys, Mama. I couldn't get up the ladder with my skirt on, but the captain is up there."

Mama smiled. "Come, Britta. Your skirt never kept you off ladders at Vistaso."

"But the rocking of the ship made it worse, Mama. Hilda fell and hit her head. I think maybe that's why she's sicker than I am."

The ship seemed to be pitching less.

Was the wind dying down, or was Britta getting used to the rocking? A few people were moving around a bit– maybe the worst of the trip was over. Britta set Lisel on the floor and wiggled her finger. The kitten pounced and tried to wrestle Britta's finger to submission. She pulled it away and wiggled it again. Elsa knelt by the kitten and giggled as it pounced on her pudgy hand.

Arvid joined them on the floor. "Let me! Let me!" he crowed. Each child took a turn teasing Lisel, who was soon rolling and pouncing between the children. Before long a group of children had gathered around, laughing and begging for a turn.

Britta beamed as the little ones played with the kitten. She peered over at Mama, who looked on with a peaceful smile. Britta scooted up to sit on the bench beside her.

Mama put her arm around Britta. "It was nice of Hilda to let you have the kitten for a while. She's helped the children get their minds off their stomachs. Me, too. She reminds me of one of the kittens we left back home."

Britta gulped.

"Are you glad to be on our way to America?" Britta asked, changing the subject. "Do you miss Papa?"

Mama smiled. "It will be good to be a family again, Britta. Your father's good humor will make our days brighter. I hate to leave

Finland, but I thank God we're all healthy. Did you see the family they left behind at Hango?"

"Oh, Mama! I felt so sorry for them. What do you think happened?"

"Someone must have been sick. They won't let people with measles or chicken pox on board."

"But Mama, we've all been sick tonight! Do we have to tell?"

"Nearly everyone's been sick, Britta. They can't leave us all behind."

Britta stayed on the bench with Mama as the pink-tinted sky grew lavender, then purple, and finally black. As the children yawned and joined their mothers, Britta bent down and fed Lisel some scraps of rye bread. She wondered where she might find some water for her but didn't have the energy to go searching for it. Britta crawled up next to Mama and rested her head against Mama's arm as she knitted and hummed.

Well into the night, someone called "Lighthouse in the distance! Land ahoy!"

Mama roused the children. "Let's go have a look."

Britta let Elsa carry Lisel as they stood at the railing to watch the distant lighthouse beam on the horizon. As the lights of a city grew brighter, more and more people gathered at the railing to watch the ship near land.

Britta's heart pounded with excitement. "We're there, Mama! We're in England, and tomorrow we'll be on our way to Papa!" she exclaimed, throwing her arms around Mama's waist. Britta's smile vanished, though, when she looked up to see tears streaming down Mama's cheeks.

"Don't worry, Britta. They're happy tears. I'm happy to be on our way, and even more happy to be done with this miserable voyage across the Baltic."

Britta didn't know what to say, so she just hugged Mama harder.

Johan appeared and announced, "We

won't leave right away. We have to take a train to Liverpool and board a huge steamship there. The captain told me."

Britta bristled. The captain told me. What a show-off! Another day of waiting. She was so very tired of waiting, waiting, waiting. She glared at Johan. He thought he knew everything. Well, he didn't. He didn't know about her kitten. She took Lisel from Elsa and stroked her silky fur.

"Don't you think you'd better find Hilda and return her kitten? You've had it for hours," Mama said.

"I guess so," Britta mumbled. She did not want to give up the kitten, but what could she do? What if they got separated in England? She would pretend to look for Hilda, then say she couldn't find her. More lying.

"I'll be back," she said and disappeared through the crowd of passengers to the other side of the ship. A sliver of moon hung over the water, casting a long, glimmering path across the sea. Papa had called it a Moon Road. Britta smiled as she remembered sitting by the pond with Papa and watching the moon rise over the water. She tried to imagine Papa beside her. It wouldn't be long now– she hoped.

CHAPTER 6
HULL, ENGLAND

When they landed at Hull, only men were allowed ashore. "Women and children stay on board until breakfast," the officers announced.

"I'm the Man of the Family, Mama. I'll go on shore and find out what will be happening. Maybe I can bring back some food for you."

"You'll do nothing of the kind, Johan. You're only thirteen years old, and if we couldn't find you on the boat, how will we ever find you in the city?" she said. "We'll go inside and wait until they tell us we can go ashore—together!" Britta turned her back to Mama and stuck her tongue out at Johan.

Johan sulked as they waited, but dawn finally came, and he led them off the ship.

Breakfast was set for them in a long room near the train station. Britta was amazed at the huge room set with long tables of bread, cheese, milk and fruit. Her mouth watered at the sight of it.

The bread was white as a cloud, and just as soft. After a quick prayer, Britta bit into it, fascinated with the new taste and texture. Her eyes sparkled as she looked across the red checkered tablecloth at Mama. "It's delicious! Do you like it?"

"It's a marvel. I didn't know how hungry I was until we sat down. And look at the boys. I think that is Arvid's third piece!"

Always the boys. Oh, well. Britta dipped a piece of bread into her milk and fed it to Lisel, who gobbled it eagerly. After filling both herself and her kitten, she scanned the huge dining room and spotted Hilda. "I'm going to say hello to Hilda and return her kitten," she announced. She bounded off through the crowd before Mama could say no.

"Hello, Hilda," she panted as she stood behind her new friend.

"Oh, Britta! Hello! Mama, Papa, this is my new friend, Britta, and this is her kitten, Lisel," Hilda said, reaching for the kitten with a wink at Britta. Her mother was a heavy woman with a round, friendly face framed in a crown of fat, brown braids. She nodded at Britta, her cheeks too full to speak.

Hilda's father stood to shake Britta's hand. "I'm glad to meet you," he said through his bushy, rust-colored beard. Light brown hair curled at his neck and around his ears, and his green eyes smiled as he spoke. So that was where Hilda got those dazzling green eyes!

After breakfast the travelers were ushered to the train. It was far nicer than the one they'd taken in Finland. The seats were soft and covered with a dark red velvety fabric. The train to Liverpool filled quickly, but Britta spotted a group of open seats.

"Oh, Mama! Could we invite Hilda and her parents to sit with us? There are enough seats for the five of us and the three of them. Please, Mama?"

"I suppose. Go find them, then, and we'll put some of our things on those seats," Mama said. "Don't be too long, and whatever you do, don't get off the train!"

"I'll help," offered Johan.

"Oh, no you won't. You're not leaving my sight until we're on the ship to America, young man. I've worried about you enough. I was sure you'd fallen into the Baltic on the crossing last night. You'll stay with me."

Britta cast Johan a taunting smile, flipped her braids over her shoulders, and waltzed off to find Hilda. That would teach him to wander off. It served him right! She hoped Mama would follow through with her threat.

Hilda and her parents were just stepping onto the train as Britta reached the end of the car. "We saved seats for you," Britta said with a smile. "Can you sit with us?"

"Oh, please, Papa?" Hilda asked, tilting her head sweetly as she nuzzled Lisel to her cheek.

"That will be fine. Show us the way, Britta," Hilda's papa said with a slight bow.

Oh my goodness, Britta thought as she led them to their seats. Now what have I done? What if our parents talk about Lisel? They'll figure it out! Suddenly, sitting together didn't seem like such a great idea.

Britta forced a smile as she introduced Hilda's parents to her family. Her heart was pounding, and not with excitement. She cast a warning glance to Hilda, who seemed unaware of their dilemma. Hilda set the kitten on the floor and began building her a nest of canvas bags and belongings piled on the floor. How could she be so calm?

Britta sat next to Mama, listening nervously to the adult conversation.

"It's a long trip for such little ones," Hilda's father said.

"Thank goodness the children have the kitten to entertain them," Hilda's mother answered.

Mama said, "She reminds me of..."

"How long until we get to Liverpool, Mama?" Britta blurted, a blush filling her cheeks. She knew better than to interrupt, but she couldn't bear for them to discover the truth about the kitten. Mama gave her a puzzled look, but said nothing.

"We should be there by dinner time," Hilda's papa answered. Then they began talking about Liverpool and the journey ahead.

Full and exhausted, Lisel lay asleep in her nest as the parents chatted quietly about memories of life in Finland and hopes for a better life in America. Britta could finally relax.

Hilda joined Britta on her bench, and they talked until their eyes drooped in the afternoon heat. Lulled by the swaying and rumbling of the train, they slept away most of the afternoon, curled together like sisters.

Britta roused once to see Mama watching them with a gentle smile, her knitting needles clicking away to the rhythm of the train.

Late that afternoon, the train pulled into the Liverpool station. Once they had gathered their things, Hilda took Britta's hand as they stepped off the train. Britta was astonished to see the vast assembly of trains lined up in the station. Towering green and red steam engines puffed smoke into a huge gray cloud that hovered above them. The air was filled with the clatter of carts, the shouts of workers, and the hubbub of emerging passengers. Britta heard people talking strange languages and wondered which one was English. Soon she would speak it, too. But how would she ever learn it?

"If we stick together, our families will

stay close," Hilda said. "We have tickets for the same ship. I heard my parents talking to your mama about it, and I think she was glad. She said it would be good to have a man to rely on. My papa can do anything!"

"Well, so can mine!" Britta snapped. She wished it was her papa and not Hilda's who was taking care of them. It felt good to have a man in charge, though. Johan would not know what to do, and Mama never asked questions. She always just did as she was told, and it didn't look like anyone in the station intended to tell them what to do. There was no order to this train station at all.

When everyone had gathered on the platform, Hilda's papa said, "I'll go check on the trunks. You wait here."

Britta set Lisel on the ground while they waited. The kitten pounced on Elsa's shoe, fighting with the knotted laces. Elsa bent to stroke her.

Arvid shoved his boot next to Elsa's, and the kitten pounced on her new prey. She climbed up his laces and tried to continue up his pale, thin leg.

"Ouch!" he cried, shaking her off. Lisel rolled onto the ground, but she seemed less disturbed than Arvid. He held up his scratched leg to show Mama, who bent to kiss it.

"Don't worry, Arvid. You'll live to see America," she laughed. Britta could see that with Hilda's family along, Mama was cheering up. She hadn't smiled so much in years. It was going to be a wonderful trip!

"What do we do next, Mama?" Britta asked. "Do we go straight to the boat?"

"I don't know, but Mr. Toikenen will find out," she answered. "We'll be on our way soon."

Britta beamed. With Hilda's papa in charge, everything would be fine. She just knew it.

CHAPTER 7
A LIVERPOOL DELAY

"Three days in Liverpool? No! I want to leave for America NOW!" Britta cried. "I want to see Papa!" Britta bit her trembling lip, but telltale tears brimmed in her eyes.

"Now listen, Britta," Mama soothed, putting an arm around her shoulder. "Life is full of problems, and we must face each one with a good heart. You have a few days to explore Liverpool, and you have Hilda and her kitten for company. Be a good girl and stop crying."

Britta shrugged Mama away. Didn't she want to see Papa? And anyway, it wasn't Hilda's kitten– it was hers!

"Don't be sad, Britta," Elsa said, petting Britta's hand. Through a haze of tears, Britta saw the concern in Elsa's blue eyes. Dear, sweet little Elsa. She felt her disappointment drain away even though she wasn't ready to let go quite yet. After all, Britta wasn't the only one. They all had to wait. Britta knelt down, and Elsa wrapped her thin arms around Britta's neck. Elsa could cheer anybody up, Britta thought.

Mr. Toikenen located a wagon for their luggage, and the two families followed it to the Union Hotel, just three blocks from the station.

The hotel lobby was filled with emigrants speaking strange languages. Britta loved the bright scarves and dark features of many of the women, and she tried not to stare at the dark-skinned people, but they were so different! America would be a strange place with people from so many countries. Were they all going to Minnesota?

"Your family has room 128," Hilda's father announced. "We're next door in room 126." He and Johan hefted the round-topped trunk up the stairs.

"Hooray!" Hilda squealed. "We can tap on the walls when we want to meet. Won't this be fun? It's my turn for Lisel, isn't it? She needs some peace and quiet for a while, and your room will be noisy." She held out her hands for the kitten.

Britta hesitated. She didn't want to give her up, but they had agreed. She lifted Lisel to her cheek and nuzzled a quick farewell. "Take good care of her, Hilda. She's probably hungry. She hasn't had anything to eat since last night."

"Oh, I will. I'll meet you in the hall later. I'll knock on the wall, and we can take her for a little walk."

Mama opened the door to their room, and Mr. Toikenen and Johan set the trunk in the middle of the floor. The room was small with a tiny window. Once-white curtains billowed in the breeze. The room had a sooty gray smell, but it looked clean. The only furniture was two narrow beds and a small wooden table in the corner with a cracked basin and pitcher for washing. A dingy mirror with a thin black frame hung on the wall over the basin. A tiny coal stove squatted in another corner with a pail of coal beside it.

"So– this will be our home for the next few days," Mama said firmly as she opened the trunk. Britta wondered if she was disappointed or just tired. "It's better than a rug in the lobby or a train seat, don't you think? Britta, help me find our quilts and make up the beds."

Mama pulled a quilt from the trunk, buried her face in it for a moment, and sighed. "It smells of home."

Britta pulled a second quilt from the trunk and said, "But Mama, our new home is America."

"Yes, America."

Britta spread her quilt over one of the beds. "I can sleep with Elsa in one bed, and you can sleep with Arvid in the other one," she suggested.

"That's a good idea, Britta. Johan will

have to sleep on the floor. He'll manage."

Britta smiled inwardly. Only fair, she thought, for The Man of the Family.

"Where's Lisel?" Elsa asked as Britta smoothed the quilt.

"She's with Hilda for a while. She needs some quiet."

Elsa frowned. "But it's our..."

"It's HER turn, and it IS her kitten, you know," Britta interrupted. She glanced at Mama, who didn't seem to be listening. Britta smoothed Elsa's hair and gave her a quick hug. "Don't worry, we'll get her back soon," she whispered, praying that they could keep their secret for three more days.

Mama stood surveying the room with hands on her hips. "The flat trunk can be our table. Mr. Toikenen told me the hotel serves breakfast and supper, and we'll use our rye bread and cheese for lunch."

Britta thought back on the long days she and Mama had spent mixing, kneading, and baking bread before they left. She'd thought it was silly to take thirty loaves along. She wondered if they could eat all that bread and the five wheels of cheese in just two weeks.

Arvid and Elsa danced happily around the trunk as Mama and Britta arranged the room. When Johan and Mr. Toikenen arrived with the flat-topped trunk, Mama opened it and pulled out a rye loaf.

"Here, Mr. Toikenen. Take a loaf of Finnish hard rye for your lunches."

"No, but thank you, Mrs. Jacobson. We brought our own bread, and you have five mouths to feed. You are very kind. God bless you," Hilda's father stepped out, closing the door behind him.

The two trunks filled the tiny room, but Britta was relieved to finally have their trunks with them. They had traveled three days without a change of clothes, a quilt, or a loaf of bread.

Mama bowed her head. "Lord, we thank you for our safe passage so far on this voyage and ask you to bless this bread that we are about to receive. We thank, you, too, for bringing Mr. Toikenen to guide us on our travels. In the name of the Father and the Son and the Holy Ghost, Amen."

"Amen," the children chorused.

Because there were no chairs, they all knelt around the flat-topped trunk, which Mama had spread with a clean cloth. Elsa's and Arvid's heads barely reached the top of the trunk, so they scrambled to their feet and stood at the "table." As they ate, Britta noticed a far-away gleam in her mother's eye. The hard rye tasted like home.

Tap-tap-tap...tap-tap-tap! Britta tapped an answer on the wall to Hilda's room, then raced to open the door and peer into the hallway. Hilda's red head peeked around the next door, and both girls giggled. Hilda beckoned for Britta to join her.

"Mama, may I please go to Hilda's for a while?" Britta asked.

"Yes, but don't be too long. Don't be a bother."

"I won't. I'll be back soon."

"Can I go, too?" Elsa piped.

Britta closed the door behind her before Mama could make her include Elsa. She wanted to be alone with her new friend. She'd invite Elsa next time.

Hilda's room was just like the Jacobsons', but there was much more space. There were only three people in their family, and their one trunk was pushed against the wall near the door. Their trunk had beautiful carving on it, and the name "Toikenen" was painted in fancy letters with a flowered border. Hilda opened the trunk and pulled out a long piece of ribbon as blue as the sky.

"This can be a leash for Lisel's Liverpool Adventure. We'll take her out on the sidewalk so she can see the city and do her business. Papa said we can walk around the block if we promise not to cross any streets. I promised we wouldn't talk to strangers. We can look in the shop windows, and with a leash Lisel can't get lost– or stolen!" she said as she tied the ribbon loosely around Lisel's neck.

"Don't you think it would be good to tie

it around her belly, too?" Britta suggested. "It might slip over her head, and if it's too tight, it might choke her."

"Good idea," Hilda said as she looped the ribbon around Lisel's belly and then around her neck. She tied it in a big bow behind her ears. "Doesn't she look cute? She's such a sweet little thing. Do you want to go for a walk, Lisel?" she crooned as she opened the door to the hallway.

"Remember– stay together, and don't cross the street," Mr. Toikenen reminded her.

"Yes, Papa. We'll remember."

"How about a kiss for Mama?" her mother said, tapping her fat cheek. Hilda obediently went to kiss her goodbye.

Hilda led Lisel down the stairs, a slow process since each step was huge to the tiny kitten. The girls giggled as Lisel tumbled over one of the long steps. She had to be coaxed to take the next step.

"Why don't we just carry her?" Britta asked.

"Oh, she needs the exercise, and this is her Big Liverpool Adventure!"

"It's our Big Liverpool Adventure, too," Britta said with an eager grin.

CHAPTER 8
LIVERPOOL ADVENTURES

Britta balked as they headed out the front door. "Are you sure we won't get lost?" she worried. The streets were so busy, and people hurried by without a glance at the two girls and their ribboned kitten.

"Don't worry!" Hilda said, "I've been to the city with my Mama lots of times. It's easy! Let's be rich American ladies visiting Liverpool." She added in a haughty voice, "We've come to shop."

"And you know..." Britta pointed her nose snobbishly skyward. "It is the fashion to have our kitten on a leash. We shall find an even finer ribbon for Lisel!"

"Look at that splendid hat, Britta! I think we should look!" Hilda pointed to a millinery shop across the street. In the center of the window perched a blue hat decorated with a brilliant peacock feather and indigo ribbons.

"But Hilda, your papa said not to cross the street."

"Oh, he'll never know. He just didn't want us to get lost. It's straight across from the hotel, and we can come right back. It's even closer than going around the block."

Britta bit her lower lip. Hilda scurried across the street with Lisel, leaving Britta at the curb.

She hated to disobey, but hadn't Hilda's papa also said they should stay together? Keeping her eyes on Hilda, Britta stepped nervously into the street. She watched Hilda to make sure she didn't disappear into the crowd before Britta reached her. Suddenly a cart whizzed by behind her, throwing her off balance. She pitched forward onto the cobblestone street. Her palms stung and her knees hurt. She looked up for Hilda.

"Britta! Watch out!" Hilda screamed as Britta saw another cart heading straight at her! She scrambled to her feet, but her boot caught in the hem of her dress and tripped her. She shrieked as the horse's hoof struck her leg. She knew it was the end for her. Oh, why had she tried to cross the street? Suddenly, her dress was yanked from behind and she fell backwards. She was still alive! Someone had pulled her out of the horses' path and out of harm's way.

Britta trembled as she looked up into the eyes of a dark-haired young man with a black top hat. He still clutched her skirt. "Th-thank you, Sir," she stammered in Swedish.

He smiled down at her and said something in a language she didn't understand. He
helped her to her feet, and as he led her to the
sidewalk he said a bit more that sounded like
scolding, though Britta had no idea what he
was saying. She hung her head to show she
was sorry, then looked up with a smile and a
nod to thank him again. He nodded back,
said one more thing, then disappeared into
the bustling crowd.

Before she knew it, Hilda was back at
her side. "Wasn't that exciting? You were
almost killed! Don't you know to look for carts
before you cross the street? Haven't you ever
been in a city? I lived near Vaasa, and we had

to be very careful when we were in town. Wasn't that man handsome? He was a shining prince. Oh, I wish I were you. I would have reached up and kissed him. Are you all right? Did you get hurt?"

Britta looked at her burning palms. They were scraped and bleeding. Her knee hurt, too. "I need to find some water to clean up," she said. "But I think I'm all right."

"Don't you want to go look at the hats?"

"No. I'm staying on this side of the street," Britta said. "We said we would, you know."

"Oh, Britta. Sometimes you're such a scaredy cat!"

Britta shrugged and continued down the sidewalk. Hilda skipped to catch up with her. They found a public fountain around the corner from the hotel, and Britta washed her hands. Her palms tingled in the cool water, but they felt much better.

"I'd like to have Lisel now, Hilda," she said.

Hilda hesitated, then handed her the leash. "You won't tell, will you?" Hilda asked as they climbed the steps to their rooms.

"Never," Britta said with a smile. "I'm your friend."

The three days in Liverpool flew by. Britta and Hilda played in the hallways, took Lisel on daily walks, and giggled their way through adventure after adventure. Hilda's papa took all the children to a nearby park each afternoon. "We'll give the mamas a moment to themselves," he said with a wink. Britta knew he enjoyed the fresh air as much as she did. The park was a welcome change from Liverpool's dreary, brick buildings. Britta loved its brilliant red and yellow blossoms, majestic elms, and neatly-clipped hedges. It was a wonderland in the dreary city.

When Britta woke on Wednesday, she pinched herself to make sure it was real. They would board their ship for America today! She trembled with excitement as she helped Mama repack the trunks. They would see Papa in just a few weeks– maybe even less. Britta hopped down the stairs holding Hilda's hand as Johan and Mr. Toikenen dragged the trunks down and loaded them onto a flat wagon.

The travelers followed the wagon to the pier, talking and laughing along the way. Mama seemed happy, and Britta could tell she was relieved to have Hilda's papa with them on this voyage. Britta was, too.

Ships of all shapes and sizes crowded the docks and the river. Everywhere Britta looked, there were more ships. Whistles and horns and toots filled the air, drowning out the chatter of the milling passengers. How would they ever find their ship?

A huge black and white ship was moored at the end of the dock, dwarfing all the others. It made their other boat, the *Arcturus*, look like a rowboat. High at the top of its masts flew an American flag– the stars and stripes! Britta shivered with delight. "Look, Hilda. That will be our flag in just a few weeks!"

"That's our ship!" Johan yelled, racing ahead. "That's the *Baltic!*"

"Johan!" Mama called, but Johan didn't stop. Britta rolled her eyes. Mama would send her to catch him. She handed Lisel to Hilda and started off.

"Johan, you get back here RIGHT NOW!" Mr. Toikenen shouted. Johan stopped in his tracks. Britta shivered. She had never heard Hilda's papa angry, and she was glad he wasn't angry with her. He'd keep Johan in tow!

The emigrants gathered in a long line to board the ship. Announcements boomed in many languages, and Britta strained to listen for Swedish over the hubbub of the crowd.

"After you pass the medical check, pick up your luggage, go through the gate and board the ship. Third class passengers line up along the fence, and cabin passengers move ahead to the gangway."

Britta's family stepped into line behind the Toikenens. "Johan, you stand behind Mr. Toikenen, and Britta and I will stand behind with the twins," Mama ordered. When Mr. Toikenen said, "Why doesn't your family go first," Mama refused.

Britta saw that most of the cabin passengers wore store-bought clothes. She admired their feathered and ribboned hats and bright traveling cloaks. She also noticed that they moved quickly through the gates, while the third class line seemed to stand still.

Suddenly a loud crashing sound filled the air. Britta whirled to see what it was. An entire cartload of trunks had overturned in the street, upsetting horses and traffic.

"Owee! Mama!" Elsa screamed then burst into sobs. Britta turned to see Mama lift Elsa into her arms.

"There, there, *Flicka*," Mama crooned as she wiped Elsa's tears. Elsa pointed to a man behind them and sobbed, "That man hit my eye with his umbrella!"

Britta glared at the man, who didn't seem to care one bit. Didn't he know what he'd done? Elsa cried onto Mama's shoulder for a very long time. Britta prayed that it was not serious.

Finally, Mama lifted Elsa's head and examined her eye, which was red and beginning to swell. "It's not bleeding," she said. "Can you open it?"

Elsa opened it a tiny bit, still whimpering. "You'll be fine," Mama soothed.

Hilda's family was ahead of them in line, and the examiner passed them through. Hilda waved back at Britta as she headed up the gangway, cuddling the kitten. She called something to Britta, but there was too much noise on the pier to hear her.

The medical examiner took one look at Elsa and waved them aside. He said many things that Britta couldn't understand, but the word "No" was loud and clear, the same in English as Swedish. He pointed to a small group off to the side, indicating that they should stand there.

"But she just got poked in the eye!" Britta protested. "Just now!" Her throat tightened and she could feel tears welling in her eyes. "Mama! Tell them!" Oh, if only she could speak English. She would make them understand! "Please listen!" she cried, and she pointed to the man's umbrella. She pantomimed being bumped in the eye, but the official ignored her. "Please! Please! Listen to me!" she cried, tugging at his jacket.

"Hush, Britta. We must do as we're told," Mama said as she pulled Britta away. "We'll get on the ship. Elsa isn't ill. Maybe this group is waiting for an interpreter." Mama hustled her family across the pier, still carrying Elsa. There was a large family standing there. The papa carried a small child wrapped in a blanket.

"Mama! We have to tell them. What if

they don't let us on? Hilda has Lisel, and Papa is waiting for us! We have to get on the ship!" Britta pleaded.

Mama stood silent, her face stony, waiting for instructions from the ship's officers. "Mama! Please ask!" she begged.

"Hush, Britta. You make things worse."

Finally Britta spotted Hilda's father walking back down the gangway. He spoke to an officer on the pier, who shook his head. Hilda's father surveyed the line of immigrants, searched the pier near the ship, took off his hat, and scratched his head.

"We're over here!" Britta cried. "Over here! Come and help us!" Britta waved her arms wildly.

A horse cart clattered by, adding to the hubbub of the crowd. He hadn't heard her! "We're over here! Wait for us! Look over here!" she cried, jumping up and down. Mr. Toikenen took another look around then turned back up the gangway. As he disappeared into the ship, Britta froze with her mouth open.

Oh, Please, God. Please get us on the ship, she prayed. Papa is waiting!

Bells gonged and whistles tooted. People shouted and waved from the deck as the Baltic pulled away from the dock.

"NO!" Britta screamed.

Other families had been rejected by the

medical examiner because of illness, but Elsa wasn't sick! She had only been bumped! No one would listen. No one cared. And Hilda and Lisel were on that ship– her only friend and her only kitten, lost forever!

Britta bit her lip and swore that this would never happen to her again– she would learn English. She felt a lump rise in her throat, and through a haze of tears she watched the ship weave its way through the busy harbor on its way to America without her.

CHAPTER 9
MORE WAITING

Britta couldn't believe it. Her worst fears had come true. They had been left behind with no man to guide them and nowhere to turn. They were truly helpless. What would they do?

"Come with me, please," a deep voice said in Swedish.

Britta looked up into the friendly gray eyes of a tall, bearded man in a dark blue uniform. Where had he been when Elsa was hurt? He could have translated for them!

Mama didn't answer, so Britta said in Swedish, "They thought there was something wrong with Elsa's eye, but there wasn't! She just got poked by an umbrella. We should be on that ship! Papa is waiting for us in America!"

"You'll have to wait for the next ship. You can stay on in the Union Hotel. There is a doctor for the White Star Line who will look at your sister's eye in the hotel lobby this afternoon. If she is well by next Wednesday, you can take that ship."

"But we have no money to pay for the hotel!" Mama said. Britta saw tears welling in her mama's eyes. Poor Mama! In her own world of hurt, Britta had forgotten how lost Mama must feel.

"Show me your tickets," the man said with a smile.

Mama handed over the packet of tickets, and he examined them carefully. "You won't have to pay. Your ticket includes transportation and lodging between Vaasa and New York. The White Star Line will cover your lodging and two meals a day during any delay for up to one month."

"How will my husband know we're not on the ship?"

"If you have an address, you can send a telegram."

"I have an address, but it's in Minnesota. Johan Erik must be on his way to New York to meet us by now." She paused a moment, then brightened. "He'll see that we're not on the ship, so he'll wait for the next one, and we'll be on it. I have waited four years. Another week will make little difference."

Britta was glad to hear the strength in Mama's voice, but she thought another week would be an eternity, especially without Hilda and Lisel.

On the way back to the hotel, Britta read English signs and tried pronounce them, even though they meant nothing to her.

"Bank ... Pub ... Bake Shoppe ... Hotel!" She knew what that meant.

Before long, they were settled back into a room at the Union Hotel, but it wasn't so fun this time. It was up six flights of stairs, but at least it had three beds.

"I want my OWN bed," Elsa whined.

"I want to go to the park," Arvid cried.

"I'm hungry," Johan said, "I want to EAT!"

"Yes, yes, yes!" Mama sighed. "Please, everyone. Be quiet."

Mama sliced bread and cheese while Britta made up the beds. They had a corner room this time, which meant two tiny windows instead of just one.

"Lord, we thank you for the food we are about to eat, and we thank you for keeping us healthy. Amen," Mama said.

"And please let us get on the next ship," Britta added.

"And please let us get on the next ship," Johan mimicked in a sing-song voice. Britta stuck out her tongue and kicked him. Mama scowled, but said nothing.

Britta wasn't hungry, but the rye bread and cheese lifted her spirits. She decided she would use every minute of this week in Liverpool to learn English.

"Johan and Britta," Mama announced, "I want you to take Arvid to the park while I bring Elsa to see the doctor."

Britta thought the doctor would be English, and maybe she could learn a few more words. "I'll stay with you, Mama, and after we're done, I'll show you and Elsa the way to the park, too."

Mama smiled. "Why thank you, Britta. That's very kind." Britta flushed, embarrassed that her selfishness was mistaken for kindness.

The gray-eyed bearded man who had guided them back to the hotel was in the lobby with the doctor, and Britta was surprised to hear him translate a few different languages for the emigrants. The people ahead of them were Swede-Finns, too. She remembered them from the Arcturus. They uncovered their baby, and its little voice was hoarse from crying. Britta peered at its tiny beet-red face.

"*Measles*," said the doctor in English. Britta memorized the English word, unsure what it meant.

She listened for the Swedish translation. "Measles."

"*Don't bring him back into the hotel.*" The doctor paused after each sentence as the bearded man repeated in Swedish. "*He should be in the hospital. At the desk they will give you taxi fare to take him to St. Mary's Hospital. Once he is well, you'll need to wait two weeks before you can board a steamer.*" Britta tried to remember everything, but her head was jumbled with the unfamiliar words.

Tears streamed down the woman's cheeks as she wrapped her baby in its embroidered blanket. The father put his arm around her, and they headed over to the reception desk.

"*Next?*" Britta memorized that word, too.

Mama pushed Elsa toward the doctor and pointed to her eye. It was hardly even pink any more.

The doctor examined Elsa's eye and smiled at Mama. "*She's fine. You can take the ship next Wednesday.*" The bearded man translated.

Before they left, Britta pulled at the sleeve of the bearded man. "Can you tell me the best way to learn English?"

"Well, *lilla flicka*, the best way is to go to school every day in America. But until then, point to things and ask '*What is this?*' and remember what you're told."

"*What is this?*" Britta repeated. "*What is this?*" Though she wasn't sure what she was saying, she would use it over and over. She smiled at the kind man. "*Tack sa mycket.*" (Thank you so much)

Britta bent over to hug Elsa. "You're just fine, Elsa. We'll be on the ship next week. Would you like to go to the park to find Johan and Arvid?"

Elsa's eye was still a little swollen as she beamed up at her big sister, "Oh, yes, yes, yes!"

As they headed off to the park, Britta announced, "I'm going to learn English starting right now. Just watch me."

"*What is this?*" she asked a woman sitting by a fruit display.

"*It's an apple,*" she said with a smile.

"*It's an apple,*" Britta repeated.

"*It's an apple,*" Elsa said. "I can say English, too!"

Mama just smiled.

The next afternoon Britta found the bearded man sitting alone in the lobby.

"*Hello,*" she said in English.

"*Hello, lilla flicka,*" he answered with a smile.

Then Britta launched into Swedish. "I'm trying to remember English words, but they're all a jumble in my head. Can you help me?" she asked.

"Well, maybe you should write them down," he said. "Can you read?"

"Yes."

"And do you have some paper?"

Britta blushed. "No"

"And I suppose no pencil either," he said.

Britta shook her head.

The man dug in his pocket and handed

her a pencil stub. "Go over to the desk and ask the man for some paper. They keep it for guests who want to write letters. The English words to say are, '*Paper, please.*' Can you do that?"

"*Paper, please,*" Britta repeated. "*Paper, please.* Oh, thank you...what is your name?"

"Siegfried," he said.

"Thank you, Mr. Siegfried."

"And your name is..."

"Britta. Britta Jacobson." She grinned, then hurried to the hotel desk, where she was given two clean white sheets of paper. She raced up to her room to write out all the words she could remember.

And so her days went. For six days, Britta worked on her English. Everywhere she went, she asked, "*What is this?*" and slowly she learned the names of things. She looked at signs and tried to sound them out using the more distinct, clean sounds of the English language. English was like music to Britta.

Each night she wrote down as many of the words as she could remember from that day, making her own personal English/Swedish dictionary. She knew her spelling wasn't right, but as she saw some of the words on signs, she crossed out the misspellings and corrected them. She talked with Siegfried using the new words she had learned, but she was too embarrassed to show him her messy, misspelled dictionary pages.

When she picked up her breakfast at the food table in the dining room, she said "*milk*" as she poured a glass of milk, "*bread*" as she chose a slice of the soft, white bread, and "*cheese*" as she sliced a piece of cheese for her bread. Sometimes Elsa and Arvid would copy her, but Johan refused. He made a point of saying the words loudly in Swedish.

"Why don't you want to speak English, Johan?" she asked.

"Why don't you want to speak English, Johan?" he mimicked.

Britta just shook her head.

Monday night Britta fell asleep dreaming of boarding their ship in two more days. She dreamed of their new home in Minnesota, with its beautiful parlor. In her dream, she was sitting too close to a hot fire. She woke up to find Elsa up against her side, her skin burning hot.

"Mama, wake up!" Britta called. "Elsa has a fever. A bad fever."

"Oh, dear God, no!" Mama gasped as she felt Elsa's forehead. She went to the basin and wet a towel to drape across her forehead. "Oh, my little one!" Mama said, cradling Elsa in her arms and rocking back and forth with her on the trunk.

"You crawl in with Arvid, Britta. I'll take Elsa."

Britta crawled in with Arvid, but she couldn't sleep. All she could think about was the ship leaving in two days. She was worried about Elsa, but she was much more worried about being left behind again. "Dear God in heaven," she prayed. "Please let us get on the ship. Make Elsa well by morning. Please!"

The next morning when Britta climbed out of bed, she looked at Mama expectantly. "Is she better?"

"I'm afraid not, Britta. I think she's worse. I'll take her to the doctor in the lobby."

"No, Mama! Don't do that! They won't let us on the ship tomorrow!" Britta said, horrified.

"And you would rather lose your little sister?"

Britta's cheeks burned, and not from a fever. Mama was right. If Elsa was ill, she had to see a doctor. But why now? Why today? It wasn't fair!

The doctor said Elsa had the measles, and she couldn't stay on in the hotel. Mama and Johan took her to St. Mary's Hospital in a horse-drawn cab while Britta stayed behind with Arvid. She couldn't even bring herself to play with him. She sat on her bed in a daze, imagining Papa waiting for them in New York. He would have to wait forever.

She dragged herself out of her gloom to fix Arvid some lunch, and later she brought him downstairs for their light supper of herring and potatoes.

Mama and Johan didn't return until evening. Mama's face was pale and expressionless.

"What happened? You missed supper!" Britta exclaimed.

"The hospital is a long ways away," Johan said, "and the cab driver didn't speak Swedish, so we couldn't tell him to wait for us. He made us pay before we got out, and he took all the money they gave us at the desk. We had to find our way back walking, and it was miles."

Britta bit back a nasty comment about Johan's foolishness. She knew he and Mama were tired and discouraged, but if she'd gone, maybe she could have used some of her new words. If only Johan weren't so stubborn about learning English!

Britta sliced bread and cheese for Johan and Mama, frustrated that this meant more waiting. All they did was wait, wait, wait. How would they get word to Papa? When would they ever leave? She knew better than to ask these questions right now.

Poor Mama. She must be so worried! She had already had three children die in Finland, and now here they were in a strange country with Elsa in the hospital.

Mama plunked down on the trunk, took Arvid into her lap and rocked him. "Your sister will be better soon, Arvid. She'll be back with us in no time."

"Oh, my God," Mama said in a trembling voice.

"What, Mama? What is it?" asked Britta.

"He's burning up," she said, laying her cheek against Arvid's forehead. "Arvid has the measles, too."

CHAPTER 10
TRAPPED IN LIVERPOOL

Could things get any worse?

The next morning, Mama asked at the hotel desk for cab fare to bring Arvid to the hospital. There was no reason to see the doctor this time. Britta hurried to find Siegfried. "Please could you teach me the English words to tell our driver at the hospital? We have to bring my brother there, and last time the driver took all the money and left." Siegfried shook his head. "Some of the drivers are not good people, Britta. I'll tell you what to do." He wrote something on a piece of paper. He said, "Hand this paper to the driver and then say, '*Wait here, please.*' And don't give him any money until you get back. He will wait."

"Wait here, please," Britta repeated. "*Wait here, please.*"

"*Taksa mika,*" she said. "*Thank you.*" The big man gave her a gentle nod, then returned to his work.

Britta and Johan climbed into the cab with Mama, who held Arvid wrapped in a quilt in spite of the warm June weather. Britta felt rich riding in the cab with its quilted leather seats, brass fittings, and windows. When the cab driver pulled his horses up before the tall, brick hospital, Britta leaned toward him and said, "*Wait here, please.*" He looked at her with a confused expression, so she said it again more slowly. "*Wait–here–please.*" He nodded. She handed him the note, then whispered to Mama, "Don't give him the money yet."

"You wait in the cab for us, Johan, to make sure he stays. We'll be back soon," Britta ordered. For once, Johan listened to her. "If he starts to drive off, yell, "*STOP!*"

"*Stop,*" Johan repeated. "*Stop. Stop.*" His first English words, Britta thought, but she didn't say it out loud. She didn't want Johan to run off.

Mama and Britta brought Arvid inside. The lobby was lined with people waiting on wooden benches, and at one end of the room a lady in a stiff striped uniform with a wide, starched cap sat at a desk. She looked up at them and said in English, "*May I help you?*"

"*No English,*" Britta said.

Mama pointed to Arvid, then held her hand to his forehead to show that he had a fever. The woman nodded and led them to a tiny room off the lobby. It had an odd, medicine smell. Mama had a faraway look in her eyes.

"Don't worry, Mama. The twins will be better before you know it, and we can take the ship for America next week." Britta forced a smile. Inside she wondered if they'd ever see Papa again.

Mama didn't answer, So Britta looked around the room and tried to memorize the English words on bottles and drawers. *"Alcohol ... Cotton balls ... Thermometers ... Sulfa ..."* Some of the words were hard to remember. And what did they mean?

Finally, a doctor checked Arvid, shook his head, and said some things in English. A nurse led them up to the boys ward, a long, white room lined with narrow beds. Mama lay Arvid on an empty bed.

"Can't he be with Elsa?" Britta asked. "I think they'd be happier together."

"This is how they do it, Britta. The boys and the girls are kept separate. It is not our place to question." She kissed Arvid on the forehead, stroked his hair, and whispered something in his ear. "Let's go see Elsa."

Britta waved goodbye to Arvid, who looked tiny and forlorn in that huge, white room of sick boys.

Mama led Britta through an endless wooden hallway to the girls' ward, another long room with nurses bustling from bed to bed, checking temperatures, bringing water, and clucking over each little girl. At least they were kind here.

Elsa lay on her cot, fast asleep. Mama stood by her a moment, then felt her forehead and said, "She still has the fever." Britta could tell that Mama expected the worst.

A nurse came over and spoke to Mama in English, but Mama shook her head.

"*No English,*" Britta said, shaking hers as well.

The nurse nodded, then stroked Elsa's fine, light hair back off her face to show her concern. Mama nodded and tried to smile. It was an empty smile, but at least it was a smile.

The next day Mama walked the long miles to the hospital to see the twins. It took her three hours each way, so there was little time to sit with the children.

"Why don't you use the thirty dollars Papa sent us for a taxi?" Britta asked. "Papa would understand."

"No. We mustn't touch that money. They won't allow us into America without it." Britta wondered about a country with such a rule. How could poor people make a better life if they didn't let them into America? It made no sense.

Some days Johan and Britta made the long walk to the hospital with Mama, but usually they stayed at the hotel. Arvid and Elsa were improving, but they couldn't seem to shake the fever, and the hospital wouldn't release them until they were well. Britta had learned, too, that they would have to wait a whole week after getting out of the hospital before they could board the ship. Time was dragging on slowly, and the days in Liverpool were hot.

Britta enjoyed seeing new travelers come into the hotel each day, listening to their excited chatter in so many different languages. Sometimes the lobby was filled with sleeping emigrants all night, but usually everyone got rooms. Each afternoon a few families trudged dejectedly back to the hotel, kept off their ship for one reason or another. It was hard to be left behind, Britta knew, but people managed. What else could they do?

Britta wondered what would have happened if they'd gotten on the ship and Elsa and Arvid had gotten the measles on the voyage. Was there a doctor on the ship? Would they have survived without a hospital?

Britta often thought about Hilda. She had probably made new friends on the ship. She smiled at the thought of Hilda surrounded by lots of other girls, especially with Lisel to attract them. How she wished she were with them! Did Hilda think about her?

She devoted herself to learning English. She had five pages in her dictionary now, covered on both sides, and Siegfried had helped her with Swedish translations for the words she didn't know. She could say a few useful things now, like *"Hello," "How do you do?" "Thank you,"* and *"Where is ...?"* She had memorized lots of new words, and she repeated them to herself over and over during her long days in the hotel.

One afternoon when Mama was at the hospital, Johan didn't come in for lunch. That wasn't like him at all. He spent most of his time outdoors, but his stomach ALWAYS brought him back. Britta waited an hour, then two, and finally decided to hunt for him. He was probably in trouble– maybe he'd gotten hurt or lost. Britta's heart pounded as she thought of it. Of course, Mama would blame her.

She headed down the block toward the park. "Have you seen my brother?" she asked a blonde man who looked Swedish. "He's nearly thirteen and has light yellow hair like me. He's wearing tan knickers and a striped red shirt."

The man shrugged and shook his head, just like everyone else. No one in Liverpool understood Swedish! She'd have to learn the English words for describing Johan. She'd ask Siegfried tomorrow.

Britta searched up one street and down another, but there was no sign of Johan. She ran through the park, hoping against hope that she'd spot his mop of unruly blonde hair, but he was nowhere to be found. She wished she knew the words to ask for help!

She raced on, desperate to find someone who could understand– someone who could help her! Britta grew more frantic each moment. Everywhere she turned, brick buildings crowded in. Shadows darkened the street, though the sun was still high in the sky. Mama would be back soon, and if no one was there, she'd be so worried! Mama always worried.

"Johan! Johan!" she called. Britta stopped at the corner, where a horse-drawn buggy careened too close, but she stepped back, remembering that day with Hilda. She'd learned about city streets all right! Britta felt so alone– she didn't belong here. No one in

Liverpool cared about immigrant children.

She had no idea where to look next. She decided to turn right and run down that street, praying that she wouldn't get lost, too. "Johan! Johan! Where are you?"

When she spotted the river, Britta's heart stopped. What if he had fallen in? Johan couldn't swim! There had been no time for swimming on the farm in Finland; they were too busy with chores. Johan spent his days tending the sheep and the cows and pulling rocks from the fields. No wonder he loved this freedom to wander through Liverpool. But he had no right to make her worry! He should think of someone besides himself for a change!

When Britta reached the wall along the river, she heard splashing. She peered over, certain it would be Johan floundering in the water. It was just a few gray geese cooling themselves in the water.

Britta raced up the next street, weaving between shoppers that milled in the market-place. A bright display of fruit caught her eye, and the shop owner was peeling an orange. The sweet scent filled the air, and Britta's mouth watered, but she rushed on. There was no time to dream of oranges. "Johan! Johan! Where are you?" she called.

She came to another corner and looked up the street. No Johan. This time she watched for speeding horse carts. Britta's face fell. If she kept running, she's surely get lost herself. The street was busy with traffic, and shoppers hurried by as Britta stood there, confused.

"Hey, Britta! Look up!"

She shaded her eyes and peered up.

Framed in sunlight, Johan balanced on the edge of a roof three stories above her. Britta gasped and clapped a hand over her mouth. He would never survive the trip to America– he'd kill himself first with his foolishness!

"Get down here this minute, Johan!" Britta planted her hands on her hips, looking as grown up as her twelve years would allow. There was no way she'd show Johan how relieved she was to see him. He scrambled down a fire escape and jumped in front of her, grinning.

"Oh, Britta. Don't be so cross. I was exploring, and it was so much fun! I sneaked an orange from a fruit cart for lunch– the man never even noticed. How can you bear to stay inside in this heat?"

"You stole an orange? Johan, how could you?" Britta was as jealous as she was disgusted. She wondered if an orange tasted as good as it smelled. "Come back to the hotel now. Mama will be back soon. She has enough to worry about without you adding to it."

"I said I'm sorry," Johan mumbled.

"And I just borrowed the orange."

"Sure, Johan. And you're going to put it back, right? I should tell Mama that you stole."

"Good idea, Britta. Tattle, tattle, tattle tail."

The children walked together through the market. Britta's mouth watered as they went by the fruit displays. She yearned for an orange. In the middle of the next block Johan tapped her on the shoulder and raced on ahead.

Britta grinned and set off after him through the maze of cobblestone streets, pigtails and apron strings flying. Johan's red shirt was easy to follow. People turned as Johan and Britta passed by– a flash of red and blue in a sea of drab Liverpool blacks and browns. Britta chased Johan up all six flights of stairs to their room, where they collapsed onto the bare wooden floor, breathless and laughing.

Late afternoon sun streamed through the narrow window onto Britta's head. Johan leaned against the trunk and asked, "Do you think Arvid and Elsa will be coming home today?"

"How would I know? They've been in that hospital long enough." Britta scrambled up to slice bread and cheese for Johan. She was a little hungry herself. "I should think they'd get well faster if they were here with us."

"Do you think Papa got our letter yet?" Johan said as he kneeled at the trunk and stuffed a slice of cheese into his mouth.

"Oh, I hope so. We really need him to send us some money. Then Mama can take the trolley to the hospital and we can buy some fresh fruit to go with our bread and cheese. I'm getting tired of fish stew every night in the hotel. I'm starving for real meat and berries and apples. I'm so tired of Liverpool!"

"It will be fun in America," Johan said through a mouthful of bread.

Britta's eyes sparkled as she imagined life in America. Papa had a house for them, and his job logging trees paid five dollars every week. Oh, to be on a boat tomorrow! As soon as Arvid and Elsa got well, they would be on their way to a new life. Papa would play his violin and Mama would sing again. They would all sing– a happy family once more. She tried to picture Papa waiting for them at the pier in New York, but she could only remember his smile and his sparkling eyes. The memory was fading too fast– but soon ...

Britta was startled from her dream by Mama's footsteps on the stairs. The door opened and Mama stood in the doorway with tears streaming down her cheeks. "They've caught the whooping cough!" she said, her voice trembling. "Oh, my God, my babies have the whooping cough." She said. She sat on the bed, buried her face in her hands, and sobbed.

Britta sat beside her and silently reached an arm over Mama's slumped shoulders. Poor Elsa. Poor Arvid. Poor Mama. Poor all of them. It felt like they'd never get to America. But she couldn't think about that now. Today she needed to pray for the twins.

CHAPTER 11
GOODBYE, UNION HOTEL

Whooping cough was very contagious, so Elsa and Arvid were quarantined at the hospital. Only Mama was allowed to visit now, and she made the long walk to the hospital nearly every day.

"Mama," Britta said as she was leaving, "we have the American dollars Papa sent us. Why don't you use those for the horse-drawn trolley? He'll be sending us more soon."

"But what if he doesn't, Britta? We can't spend that money. Walking to the hospital gives me something to do with these long days. The day we get more money is the day I can think about the trolley."

That morning Britta sat alone in the room poring over her English dictionary. She wiped sweaty hair from her forehead as she talked to herself. "*Orange ... Apple ... Potato ... Chicken.*" Her mouth watered. She imagined a banquet of roast goose and vegetables and mashed potatoes with gravy– in English, of course. Suddenly, she was startled out of her reverie by a knock on the door. Johan and Mama never knocked, so who could it be? Her heart pounded. Should she answer to a stranger?

"*Ja?*" she said, opening the door just a crack. Britta peered around it to see Siegfried standing stiffly in the hall. She crowed with delight, threw the door wide, then said in careful English, "*Hell-o, Siegfried. Good morning.*"

"Hello, *lilla flicka*," he said, but he was not smiling. Britta knew something was wrong. Suddenly she felt shy. She stood quietly, holding her breath as she waited for his news.

"Is your mother here?"

"She went to the hospital," Britta answered.

"I am sorry, but I have some bad news," Siegfried said. "You have been in the hotel for four weeks now, and your time has run out. You must tell your mother that the fee for this room is one pound per week. If you want to stay on, you will have to pay."

Britta looked around the room, and her eyes filled with tears. "But we can't. We only have our thirty dollars to get into America. Mama says we can't spend it. What can we do?"

"I'm sorry, *lilla flicka*. There is nothing to be done. If you can't pay for the room, you must move out tomorrow. Many travelers are coming every day, and they need this room. The White Star Line pays only for one month's lodging with your ticket. Tell your mother I am very sorry." Siegfried turned and walked stiffly down the hallway. Britta closed the door and crumpled to the floor, tears streaming down her face. She wasn't interested in her English dictionary any more. She wasn't interested in anything. Life was too horrible!

When Johan came in for lunch, he saw how sad she was. "What's wrong, Britta?"

Britta sliced their bread and cheese without a word. Her face was flushed from crying, and she had to bite her lip to hold back the tears. Finally she mustered the strength to tell him the bad news.

Johan chewed on a bite of bread as he thought a moment, then his face brightened. "Don't worry, Britta. I have an idea. I was exploring by the railway yard last week, and there are some old train cars pushed over to the side. I saw people going in and out of them, and I'll bet they live there. Let's go see if there's an empty one."

Britta wasn't so sure she wanted to live in an old railroad car, but what other choice did they have? They couldn't afford to stay on in the hotel, and it had to be better than the streets. "Can we look this afternoon?"

"Sure!" Johan said, gathering up the last few pieces of bread and cheese. "I'll show you right now. It's a long ways, but we can find it."

After an endless, hot walk, Johan and Britta found the railway yard. A run-down group of old cars sat off to the side of the railroad yard, and Johan had been right. There were people living in them, emigrants like themselves. Johan and Britta peered in one after the other, and finally they found an empty one. They stepped up on an old wooden box that served as a step, and climbed inside. Once her eyes got used to the darkness, Britta realized it wasn't as bad as she'd feared. It was a little dirty, but there were a few old cots to sleep on, a tiny coal stove in the center, and a makeshift table on one end with four wooden crates for seats. It was a boxcar, so there were no windows, but it was clear that it had been lived in, and quite recently.

"We could make this nice with just a little work," Britta announced.

"Why bother? We'll be leaving in just a few days, anyway," Johan said. "It will be fine just like this. I hope nobody takes it before we can bring Mama back here."

Britta talked all the way back to the hotel about how they could make the railroad car comfortable. She thought they might hang some bright linens on the walls and wash down the floor. Maybe a few wildflowers would brighten it up, too.

They got back to the hotel before Mama returned from the hospital. As soon as she came in the door, Britta blurted, "Mama, we have to leave the hotel. If we want to stay here, we have to pay one pound a week– but don't worry..."

"We have a place to live!" interrupted Johan. "And I found it, too! It's even closer to the hospital, so you won't have to walk so far."

At first Mama was silent. She looked confused, then surprised, then relieved, all in just a few moments.

"What would I do without you, Johan?" Mama said as she reached out to hug him. "My little man."

Britta's eyes stung. She was the one who was home to get the news. She was the one who would clean the railroad car and make it home, but Johan was the one who got the praise. Always Johan! She turned away and stood by the window so no one could see her tears.

CHAPTER 12
MOVING HOUSE

The next morning, instead of heading off for the hospital, Mama got them busy packing everything up. "No exploring today, Johan," she said. "I need your strong arms for heavy work."

"Johan, Johan, Johan," Britta mumbled as she folded and packed the linens. "Johan, Johan, Johan. I wish I never heard that name!" She stuck her tongue out at him, but she wasn't sure he even noticed.

It took forever for the three of them to drag the first trunk to the railroad yard. They struggled together block after block, stopping many times to rest. People stared at them, but no one offered to help. Britta was relieved to see that their railroad car was still vacant, and she wanted to get busy cleaning, but they had to go back for the other trunk. By the time they had moved everything into the railroad car, they were too exhausted to worry about how dirty it was. "Tomorrow is another day," Mama said. "I'll go visit the twins, and

you two can make our new home clean as a whistle." She set out some sliced cheese and rye, then they all collapsed on the hard cots.

The next morning Mama fashioned a mop out of a stick and an old rag, and she sent Johan to fill their wooden bowl with water from the street fountain. "When he gets back, you two mop the floor. It's been clean before, and it will clean up just fine," she said, but without much energy in her voice. Britta could tell Mama was tired as she trudged off to the hospital. As soon as Johan came back with the water, he ran off. Britta sighed. How like him to disappear as soon as Mama was gone.

Once she had scrubbed out the railway

car, it wasn't so bad. Sunshine streamed in the open doors, and there was more space than they'd had in their hotel room.

Britta decided to walk to the hotel to see if they had a letter from Papa. She would go there every day, and then she could also talk to Siegfried and ask him about any new English words she had heard. She wondered if he had noticed that she was gone.

When Britta stopped at the hotel, she found Siegfried right away and asked him to check for mail. He came back holding an envelope in his hand. "A letter for you from America."

Britta wanted to jump up and throw her arms around him. She resisted, although she grinned from ear to ear. *"Oh, thank you, Siegfried! Thank you! Thank you! Thank you!"*

She looked at the return address. It was from Papa! It was addressed to Maria Kvevlander Jacobson at the Union Hotel, but only to Mama– no children's names. Britta knew that without her name on the letter, she would have to wait to open it until Mama got back.

She raced back to their railroad car and propped the letter on the trunk where she could keep an eye on it until Mama returned. She stared at it, hoping it was full of money for fresh food at the market– maybe even some candy!

Maybe there would be enough money to buy a blue-ribboned bonnet for the trip to America! They could buy one for her and a little one for Elsa– and one for Mama, too. Of course, Mama would probably prefer to use her part of the money for a trolley to the hospital each day. And what about Johan? They could buy him a watch to remind him to come home on time. Britta smiled. What Johan should get is a rope to tie him to their railroad car!

Before long, Mama clambered up the step into the car. Loose strands of wet hair clung to her red cheeks. She stood against the wall fanning her face. "My goodness, it's hot today." Britta noticed how Mama had grown thinner. Her dress hung loose on her narrow frame.

"How are Elsa and Arvid?" Britta asked.

"Still the same. They lay like limp dolls on their beds, straining to breathe. Oh, Britta. They're so lonely for each other and for you and for Johan!"

Britta held up the letter, and Mama's eyes brightened. "A letter from your Papa?"

"Yes, Mama!"

"So open it and read it to me!" Mama's voice had a note of excitement that Britta hadn't heard in weeks. She sat on a cot with her hands folded and her head bowed as Britta read to her.

June 10, 1904

My beloved wife and children,

I thank the Lord that you are all alive. You were not on the boat of May the 20th, and I told myself you had been delayed. I met the boat from Liverpool the next week. When you were not on that boat, I began to worry. When you were not on the third boat, I feared greatly in my heart that I was alone in the world. A man from that boat found me and gave me your letter. I was greatly relieved. I'm sad to hear that the little ones got the measles. I hope that when you get this letter, they are well and you will be waiting to depart from Liverpool. I hope you are already on a ship as I write.

My money was nearly gone by my second week in New York. I moved out of the Salvation Army Hotel and took a small room in a house near the docks. I also found employment in the shipyards. It is very hard on my back, but it is good pay. I wish I could send you more money, but this is all I have. I have changed it to British pounds for you. I will meet every boat from Liverpool. I pray each week that you will be on that boat.

America is a wonderful country. It will be good to have our family together again.

Your loving husband and father,
Johan Erik Jacobson

Britta found two one-pound notes in

the envelope. Not enough for bonnets or a watch or even ribbons. Her heart sank. "You take one for trolley fare, Mama, and I'll use the other one for food in the market. Then we can have fresh fruit each day, and you can be back in time to eat lunch with us."

"That's a good idea. If I take the trolley, I can be off the streets before the noon heat. Summer is hot here in Liverpool," Mama said. "Can you find out for me how to take the trolley? How much does it cost?"

"I'll ask Siegfried tomorrow, Mama, and I'll teach you the English words for it, too!"

The next morning after Mama left for the hospital, Britta put the two pounds in her pocket and headed for the hotel, where Siegfried helped her change it to 200 pence. If she gave half the money to Mama, she thought, she would have 100 pence left. She could spend two pence a day, and it would last for 50 days. They would never be in Liverpool that long. The twins would be coming home any day now.

Every day Britta scoured the market for bargains. None of the street vendors spoke Swedish, but she soon learned that if she held up a tupence and pointed, they understood. Tupence could buy a few potatoes, an apple, or some milk. Once, she even got an orange for them to share. It tasted like sunshine.

Britta would make their money last–

somehow. She would keep them all healthy until they could leave for America.

One gloomy, misty day in late June, the markets were not quite so busy. Britta spotted a basket of spoiled fruits and vegetables next to a display table. There were apples with brown spots, wilted lettuce, dark bananas, and shriveled squash. When she pointed to the basket and held up her tupence, the woman shook her head and set it behind the table. It was not for sale. Britta nodded eagerly, pointed again and said, *"How much please?"*

The woman, still shaking her head, picked up the basket and pointed to Britta's apron.

"Apron?" Britta asked.

"Yes!" The woman smiled and lifted the corners of her own apron to show Britta what to do. When Britta lifted her apron, the woman dumped the entire basket of spoiled fruits and vegetables into it. Britta's eyes grew wide, and her mouth dropped open. The woman took Britta's tupence and, still smiling, gave her a penny back. Britta said, *"Thank you!"* and grinned. Then she raced back to the railroad car to salvage what she could from her treasure.

That day they feasted on fresh vegetables and bits of fresh fruit with their rye bread. "My goodness, Britta. You are a wonder!" Mama exclaimed. "I hope you didn't spend too much money. We only have two pounds, and it's going fast."

Britta beamed. "One penny, Mama. All this for only a penny! I made a new friend in the market and she sold me all the spoiled things, and I sorted through them for what was still good to eat. Isn't that wonderful, Mama?"

Johan scowled. "It's about time we got some decent food around here," he grumbled. Britta laughed and gave him a playful punch in the arm. He sneered, but he didn't hit her back.

The next morning Britta visited her new friend, who filled her apron again with spoiling fruits and vegetables for a penny.

"*Thank you,*" Britta said in English.

"*You're very welcome,*" the woman chuckled, her green eyes dancing. "*Have a tart,*" the woman said, adding a miniature berry pie to the pile in Britta's apron.

Britta grinned, then repeated, "*Tart. Thank you.*"

"*What is your name?*" the woman asked.

"*My name Britta.*"

"*And my name is Sarah. Sarah Goode.*"

"*Thank you, Sarah Goode.*" Britta nodded, then skipped back to the railroad car, eager to taste the delicious-looking treat. She was tempted to devour it all herself, but she cut it into three even pieces and ate only one.

It was heaven. The berries reminded her of Finland, but the crust was a new taste– so light it melted in her mouth.

Each day Sarah Goode taught Britta a new word, helping her practice until she could say it right. English was such fun! Britta chanted her new words as she skipped back to the railroad car each day with an apron full of fruits and vegetables. Before she fixed lunch, though, she always scrawled the new words into the pages of her English dictionary.

CHAPTER 13
A LIVERPOOL GEM

Britta marked off the last day of June on her homemade English calendar. It had been two months since they had left Vistaso, and she was no nearer to America– or Papa. Siegfried had given her more paper, so she started drawing a calendar for July, checking her dictionary for the spelling she'd learned from Sarah. Her dictionary was now twelve pages long, and she had memorized the words for many things, but she still couldn't make a real sentence.

"Why do you waste all your time indoors, Britta? It's nicer outside, and there is so much to see in Liverpool. Why don't you come with me today? Do you want to see a huge, beautiful building?" Johan asked.

"I have to finish my calendar first, then go to the market."

"Come on, Britta. Just this once? We'll stop at the market on the way back. Don't be such a bore!"

"I'm learning and I'm working, which is

a lot more than I can say for you!" Britta snapped.

"I'm learning, too! I'm learning about Liverpool and about all the jobs a man can do in a city. There are cab drivers and milkmen and garbage haulers and dock workers. And the docks, Britta! I love watching the big ships come and go. Someday I'm going to be a ship's captain. You'll see. I'm NOT wasting my time! Come and try learning my way today." Johan's eyes narrowed. "Maybe you'll EVEN find some new English words."

Britta hesitated. She hadn't spent any time with Johan, and it was deathly hot in the railroad car. It might be nice to see something new. She gathered up her papers and stored them neatly in the round-topped trunk, brushed off her apron, and counted out ten pennies from the money cup– just in case.

Johan led Britta up long blocks in the Liverpool heat, and she was soon soaked with sweat. "Where is it, Johan? I'm not going much further."

"It's not far now," he said, leading her across a busy street. "Come on."

When they finally emerged from the maze of brick buildings onto a vast open square, Britta's gaze was drawn upward. A magnificent building with hundreds of tall pillars stretched to the sky. This white building was the biggest, most beautiful thing she had ever seen. God must have flown it down straight from heaven!

"My goodness, Johan. How did you find this?" she gasped.

"It was easy. I spotted it from a rooftop, and I just kept climbing buildings to follow it. Want to go inside?"

"Inside? Can we?"

"Of course, silly. It's a public building, and I think it might be a church. Churches are for everyone, rich and poor people," Johan said, leading her by the hand. Pigeons flapped up in front of them as they made their way across the square, and Britta kept tripping because she couldn't take her eyes off the huge, gold-gilt doors. As soon as they stepped inside, cool air surrounded them. People bustled in every direction, but there was a respectful hush to their voices. Britta's gaze lifted up the huge pillars running along both sides of the endless, beautiful hall. High above the pillars was an ornate, yellow ceiling decorated with brilliant panels in deep reds, golds, and browns.

Britta's eyes rested on a huge set of ornate pipes at the end of the room. "What's that?" she asked Johan.

"It's an organ, silly. Look at the little piano down at the bottom. All those pipes play music. I was here once when someone was playing it, and it fills this entire room with music. Like heaven."

"Oh, my goodness!" Britta sighed as she

walked down the long room to look at it more closely. Each pipe was carved with ornate designs, and some of them were as large as trees. Gold decorations shimmered in the mid-day light streaming from the long room's high windows.

Britta shivered. She was in heaven! No other building in the world could be this beautiful. Even the floor was beautiful, with intricate designs in gold, brown, and white tiles.

As they stepped out into the bright morning sun, Britta asked a man at the door, *"What is this?"*

"Why, Luv, it's the great St. George's Hall!" he answered with a sweeping bow.

"St. George's Hall," Britta repeated. "St. George's Hall." This name would certainly find its way into her dictionary! At the bottom of the stairs, a wrinkled old lady held out her hand to Britta and croaked something in English. Britta's heart was so full, she dug into her pocket and pulled out two pennies to place in the old woman's palm. Suddenly they were swarmed by beggars pushing open palms into their faces. Johan grabbed Britta's hand and raced with her across the plaza to escape the horde. The children stopped at the edge of the plaza, laughing as they used to after a race in Finland.

"Why did you give that old woman our money, Britta? We're as poor as she is."

"I don't know. I just did. And do you know what else? Instead of buying vegetables and fruit today, I think we should buy some candy!"

Johan stared at her wide-eyed. "I know just the place!" he said, then led her down a narrow, crowded street to a tiny store with "*Sadie's Sweet Shoppe*" painted on the window. A bell tinkled as they opened the door, and they marveled at the shelves of candies and cakes. After drooling over the bright displays, they each greedily selected a penny-weight of candy. Britta selected long-lasting hard candies, while Johan chose chewy things like chocolates and caramels. Their hearts pounded with excitement as they raced back to the railroad yard with their treasures.

They laid out their candy on the trunk and admired it. "Let's have just one before lunch and save the rest for later," Britta suggested.

"Good idea," said Johan, popping a chocolate drop into his mouth. It was gone in an instant, and he eyed Britta's cinnamon stick, which she had only begun to lick. "Could I have just a taste?" he asked.

Britta shook her head and smiled. "A penny each, Johan."

Johan scowled at her and popped two more chocolate drops in his mouth. Then he wrapped the rest of his candy back into its waxy paper and twisted the top.

Britta was startled to hear Mama's voice calling to them from outside. She didn't have a lunch ready! She quickly gathered her candies and twisted them into her paper. She and Johan stepped to the doorway, and there stood Mama, smiling, with a pale little boy in her arms. His wide blue eyes settled on Britta.

"Arvid!" she cried as she jumped down from the doorway. She lifted him from her mother's arms and squeezed him to her chest. He was skin and bones, as light as a feather. "Oh, it's so good to have you back!" She tousled his fine, blonde curls and kissed each pale cheek. "Now we can leave for America! Papa will be so proud to see what a big boy you've grown into!" Arvid wriggled out of Britta's arms and ran to greet Johan.

Britta peered behind her mother's skirts. "And Elsa?" she asked.

"I'm afraid we can't leave yet, Britta. Elsa is worse. She's caught pneumonia." With a long, weary sigh, Mama climbed up into the railroad car. When the children stepped in, they found her sitting on her cot with her head bowed in her hands. "I don't know what to do. We'll have to go back to Finland if we can't leave soon. Our money is nearly gone."

Britta gulped. She had just wasted four whole pennies.

"No, Mama. We won't go back to Finland. Papa is waiting for us, and we'll get to America if it takes forever!"

Britta pulled out a rye loaf and sliced thick slabs for each of them.

It is taking forever, she thought, her heart sinking lower than low.

CHAPTER 14
ELSA

Britta threw herself into learning English, and she taught some of her words to Arvid. He was a quick learner and she made up games to help him remember. Johan might not want to speak English, but she and Arvid would arrive in America already speaking it. She started taking Arvid with her to the market each day, and she made a game of learning words with Sarah Goode. Britta and Arvid jumped up and down, then Britta asked, "*What is this?*" Arvid repeated, "*What is this?*"

"*Jump!*" Sarah Goode laughed. "*It means jump, luv,*" and she patted Arvid's curls.

The next day Britta asked, "*What is this?*" as she and Arvid raced back and forth along the street.

"*Run, it is. Run!*" Sarah Goode laughed. "*And this is NOD,*" she added, nodding her head up and down again and again.

"*Nod,*" Britta repeated. "*Nod head.*"

"*Yes!*" Sarah had exclaimed. "*Nod your head!*" she said pointing at Arvid, who nodded his head and said, "*Nod head.*" Britta and Sarah both laughed. Learning English was even more fun with Arvid.

Britta's English words were finally becoming phrases. She tried to teach Johan and Mama some of her words, but they were always too busy or too tired. Couldn't they see how important it was? If they'd known English, they could have explained about Elsa's eye, and they would already be in America.

Johan helped Britta draw a map of the area around the Union Hotel, and she wrote English labels for the streets and the buildings and the shops and the park. If she didn't know what something was, she would ask someone, "*What is this?*" Sometimes they looked at her like she was crazy, but most people were helpful when she tried to speak English. Most of them called her "*Luv,*" which she entered in her dictionary as English for "girl."

As she prepared their lunch each day, Britta made up stories about America for Arvid. "We'll have our own fat cows and more milk and butter and cream than we can ever eat! We'll all be very plump and happy. We'll have horses and chickens, and when you get older, you'll have your own gun for hunting. And we'll all go to school every day– even the girls!" she beamed. "And Papa will take us to town in the wagon each week, and we'll buy bags and bags of candy and fruit to eat– and new store-bought clothes, too!"

Each noon when Mama returned from the hospital, Britta asked, "How is Elsa?"

Mama would report, "The same," or "Worse," but she never said, "Better." Britta could hardly remember the last time Mama had smiled. Her face grew longer and her eyes grew sadder each day.

Britta worried about Elsa, but worse than that, she was beginning to lose hope that they would ever get to America. Maybe Mama was right and they'd have to return to Finland. She prayed that Papa would keep waiting for them. He had been waiting in New York for nearly as long as they'd been away from Finland– almost three months.

She repeated her silent prayer over and over. "Dear God, Please bring us to Papa in America. Soon! Amen."

One day Mama shuffled into the railroad car with empty staring eyes. "Elsa is worse. They have her in a tent so she can breathe, and they won't even let me see her. My poor baby must be so lonely..."

Britta made Mama a cup of tea and watched her hand shake as she lifted the teacup to her lips. Wisps of hair hung in her face, and her skin looked gray. Britta sat next to Mama and rubbed her back. She could feel every rib through her dress.

"Elsa will get well, Mama. She's strong. Remember when she had the fever in Finland? Her little head was as hot as an iron, and she was out of bed in no time."

"I hope so, Britta," Mama sighed. "I do hope so."

"Things will be better in America, Mama. We'll all be healthier and happier there– and we'll be with Papa again! We can leave as soon as they let Elsa out of the hospital; you'll see."

Mama nodded. She took Britta's hand in hers. "I hope to God that you are right." Still clutching Britta's hand, she bowed her head in a silent prayer.

Britta had her own prayer, which she repeated in her mind a hundred times a day: "Dear God, Please bring us all safely to Papa in America. And soon. Amen." It was a hasty prayer, but she knew God understood.

Each day Arvid grew stronger. His pale cheeks had tanned, and he was getting some flesh back on his bones. Johan took him to the park every afternoon to play in the summer sunshine while Britta worked on her English in the shade of the railroad car. She liked to have the doors open on both sides so a breeze would flow through and cool her off. Britta was thankful that with Arvid to watch, Johan couldn't wander all over Liverpool and get lost.

Then it happened.

One muggy day in late July, all three children were sitting in the railroad car when Mama returned from the hospital early. She shuffled into the doorway, and as soon as she saw Britta she opened her mouth wide in a heart-wrenching moan. She looked hollow, like an empty husk. Tears streamed down her cheeks.

Britta ran to her.

"No, Mama! No!"

Mother and daughter sobbed in each other's arms. Between sobs, Mama whispered in a hollow voice, "She was so alone ... She died of loneliness ... She's with God now ... She won't be lonely ..."

Britta led Mama to the trunk and sat beside her, wiping her own tears with the back of her hand.

Johan took Mama's hand and held it quietly. Arvid crawled into her lap, peering up into her vacant face. Though he was too young to understand, he knew something terrible had happened. Time stood still as the dark railroad car was engulfed in sobs.

Britta's stomach felt hollow. She remembered Mama's tears after little Solveig died– but she hadn't really understood it then. She remembered tears and a tiny coffin, but not the hurt or the emptiness. Death was worse when you understood.

After Britta's tears were spent, she whispered, "What do we do now, Mama?"

"We must bury her. Then we will leave for America," Mama answered in a wooden voice. "The boat tickets are in the bottom of the trunk with our thirty dollars for America. We don't even have money for a coffin."

"I'll talk to my friend Siegfried. Maybe he can help us," Britta offered.

"Yes," Mama answered. "You do that."

"I want to come, too" Arvid said, climbing down from Mama's lap. Britta took his hand and led him toward the door.

"We'll be right back, Mama."

Mama sat still as stone, tears dripping onto her folded hands.

"Stay with Mama, Johan," Britta said as she stepped down from the railroad car. She looked back to see Johan sitting beside Mama with his arm around her shoulders.

On a dreary, drizzly day, Mama, Johan, Britta, and Arvid stood together in a cramped graveyard to bid farewell to Elsa. They watched as the small wooden coffin was lowered into the ground and a man said a few words in English. Britta understood only a little of what he said, but she was thankful Siegfried had helped them arrange a charity burial. There would be no gravestone, but Britta didn't think it would matter since they

would never want to visit Liverpool again.

Mama dropped a rose onto the coffin, and each of the children added a blossom they had selected from the park. Then Mama threw down a handful of dirt, saying, "Go with God, my precious Elsa. Go with God."

Britta's heart felt as empty and gray as the day around them. She hoped she'd never see Liverpool again as long as she lived. These months had been a nightmare.

Holding hands, Mama and her three remaining children walked silently back to their railroad car.

Britta gulped back a flutter of excitement about leaving Liverpool. She would think about it tomorrow. Today, July 25th, 1904, was a day of sadness.

Tomorrow the sun could shine. They would be leaving for America.

CHAPTER 15
THE BIG SHIP

Thanks to Siegfried, the hotel's luggage wagon stopped to pick up their trunks at the railway station, so they only had to drag them a short distance from their car. When they arrived at the docks, swooping gulls and crowds of people welcomed them. Their family was smaller this time by one little girl and one little kitten, but they were ready to leave for America. Britta bit her lip as they stepped into line, remembering the day three months ago when they had been turned away. Not this time!

"Let me go first, Mama. I can speak to them in English," Britta offered.

Mama, gripping Arvid's hand, looked back at Johan. "Yes, that would be best, Britta. We can't be left behind again."

Johan glared at Britta. "I'm The Man of the Family," he said through clenched teeth. Britta flashed him a syrupy smile and fluttered her eyes.

"You stand with Britta then, Johan.

You can hold the tickets." Mama said, handing the brown envelope to Johan.

Britta's eyes narrowed. What a brat he was. When Johan stepped beside her, she turned her back to him and focused her attention on the ship.

It was HUGE! This ship was even bigger than the other one. It had two mammoth black smokestacks slanting back from the deck, and at least a thousand portholes. And there were one, two, three, four– five levels! Black smoke drifted up from the smokestacks, swirling into the gray haze above the harbor. She read the name of the ship on its bow: *The Baltic.* The harbor was choked with boats: masted cutters, steamships of every size and shape, tugboats, and tiny rowboats. Britta wondered how *The Baltic* would make its way through all those smaller boats.

She imagined the big ship bouncing them aside as it churned toward the open sea, just as the big rock parted the water that danced in her little stream back home. Finland seemed so long ago now– a part of her life that was only a dream.

Johan poked Britta out of her reverie. They were at the front of the line, and the medical examiner was asking questions.

"*Do you speak English?*" he asked Johan.

"*A little English,*" Britta replied.

The man turned to Britta. "*Has anyone*

been sick in the last month?" he asked.

Britta wasn't sure what he'd said, but she knew the word sick. *"No,"* she replied.

"Any fever in the past week?"

"No."

"Where will you settle in America?"

"Where," she thought, racking her brain for what he meant. Oh, yes! *"Minnesota."*

"How much money do you have?"

"Thirty dollars."

He checked everyone's eyes and ears and felt their foreheads. He took a few extra moments with Arvid, and Britta's heart pounded. They would NOT be kept back! *"Arvid is good,"* she said. *"Small– not sick."* The man nodded, then pointed to an officer sitting at a table with a huge ledger before him.

Britta walked confidently up to him and smiled. *"Hello."*

"Hello, luv. Do you have your family's tickets and passports?" Britta nudged Johan to hand over the packet. The man looked at their tickets, stamped each one, and wrote their names in a ledger. *"There's one missing,"* he said. *"You have five names here."*

"Dead," Britta said, biting her lip. She swallowed hard, choking back a sob.

"Oh, I'm sorry," he said. He did seem truly sorry, too. Britta wished she could tell him more. She wanted to tell him about their long months in Liverpool as Arvid and Elsa

lay in hospital beds. She wanted to tell him about the agony of burying Elsa in a charity grave. But she didn't have the words. Not enough English words. She nodded.

"*Get your luggage and bring it on the ship.*" Britta had no idea what he'd said, but when he pointed to a pile of trunks and duffels, she nodded again.

"*Thank you,*" she said, forcing a smile.

"*Have a good trip,*" the man said, then turned to the next family.

"You did well, Britta," Mama said, giving her a quick squeeze as they headed toward the luggage. "You make me proud."

Even though she hadn't understood most of what had been said, Britta grinned. She had known enough English words to get them through. When Mama started toward the mound of trunks and duffels, Britta said, "Johan and I can get the trunks, Mama. You take Arvid up on the deck and wait for us." She looked at Johan, prepared for a sneer or a punch.

"Yes. We'll carry them, Mama," he said importantly.

Britta surveyed her older brother carefully. She didn't trust his cooperation.

Mama hesitated, then nodded. "Thank you, children."

Britta and Johan searched through the huge jumble of trunks and found theirs. First they dragged the flat-topped trunk up the long gangway, then they raced back down for the other one. Both trunks were lighter without the loaves of rye bread and cheeses. Britta hoped they wouldn't go hungry on the voyage, but she wouldn't worry about that now. They were finally on their way, and that was all that mattered. Siegfried had told her there would be food for them on the ship. No more worries about feeding the family. No more worries about being sent back to Finland. No more worries at all.

Or so she thought.

They gathered on the deck and looked down on the Liverpool pier, finally behind them forever. Men heaved boxes and bales onto their backs and hauled them up the ship's lower gangway. Carriages and carts clattered along the cobblestones delivering more passengers and trunks. People milled about while others stood in endless lines to get on the ship. Yells and bells and booming whistles filled the air. Britta's blue eyes sparkled with anticipation. Johan started toward the front of the deck, but Mama called him back.

"Not yet, Johan. You will stay with me until we leave the pier. First we must find our room," Mama said.

Following the mass of emigrants, they dragged their trunks down six flights of stairs to a huge, long room. A man stood at the entry checking tickets and directing people to certain areas. *"Single men to the left, single women to the far right, and families to the near right. Find yourself a free bunk and settle in."* He repeated this in many different languages, including Swedish.

"Oh, dear," Mama said. "I'd hoped for a room to ourselves."

"This is third class, Mama– steerage," Johan explained. "All in one room."

Britta wondered how he had learned this. She hadn't known, and she was the one who spoke English.

The vast, long room had whitewashed walls with bunk beds stacked three high against the sides. Above each top bunk was an open porthole that let in light and the sounds and smells of the harbor. Down the center of the room were long wooden tables with benches. Black pot-bellied stoves squatted between the tables, and kerosene lanterns hung from hooks in the ceiling. Great brass spittoons were spaced regularly along the floor near the bunks. Britta wondered why there were so many spittoons in the family section. Weren't they only for men?

"I'll take the top bunk!" Johan called, jumping up on one and sticking his head out the porthole.

Mama smiled indulgently. "It's only fair since you've had the floor for all these months."

"And can I have the middle one, Mama? I'll share it with Arvid," Britta offered.

"We'll take turns with Arvid, Britta. He can sleep with you tonight and with me tomorrow. I don't want him on the top bunk, though, in case he falls out."

Britta and Mama arranged their two trunks near the bunk to define a space, and Johan pulled Arvid up to the top bunk to peer out the porthole.

"Can we go back up on the deck now, Mama?" Johan asked.

"Not yet, Johan. We need to make this our home first. Get down from that bunk and you can explore down here while Britta helps me with the quilts. And take Arvid with you," Mama ordered.

Britta wished she could explore, too, but Mama needed her. They lay their bright handmade quilts out on the three bunks, and Mama pulled out the red and blue rag rug she had made for America and lay it on the floor next to their bunks. Finally, she spread her embroidered tablecloth over their flat trunk.

Britta stepped back to survey their work. "It's lovely, Mama. I think anyone going by is going to know we're Scandinavians. They won't be sure whether we're Swedes or Finns, though, and won't they be surprised to talk to us and learn that we're Swede-Finns! I wonder if there are many others on this ship.

I hope so!"

"Oh, I'm sure, Britta." Mama yawned and stretched out on the lower bunk.

"Mama, how can you lie down now? We'll have weeks to do that and little else. Can't we go up on the deck?" Britta asked.

"We'll go when the boys get back," Mama said, closing her eyes.

"Are you OK, Mama?" Britta asked, stroking her shoulder.

"I'm fine, Britta. Just tired. It's been a long summer."

"I'm sorry, Mama."

"I'm sorry too, but now it's time to leave it behind us."

Poor Mama, Britta thought. If only they'd known English, none of this would have happened. They wouldn't have been left behind, the twins wouldn't have been put in the hospital, and Elsa would still be with them.

She rummaged in the round-topped trunk for her dictionary and set it on top of all their clothes and linens. She clucked her tongue when she saw all the winter clothes they had packed. No need for them in this hot weather.

When the boys got back, Arvid exclaimed, "You have to see the W.C., Britta! There's water running right through it all the time!"

Suddenly a loud horn boomed through

the ship. "I'll see it later, Arvid. It's time for the ship to leave. Let's go up on the deck! Come on, Mama!" Britta urged.

When they got there, Britta was astonished at the mob of passengers. The children pushed their way to the railing with Mama following close behind. There were more people on this ship than Britta had ever seen in one place! There were hundreds of people speaking hundreds of different languages. How would she ever find a friend who spoke Swedish?

They watched the ship hands pull up the gangways, and the ship's horn made three great, booming blasts. Gongs sounded as the ship slowly pulled away from the dock.

Britta had never felt so glad to say goodbye.

"Goodbye forever, Liverpool, England!" she called.

Beside her, Mama stood holding Arvid as tears streamed down her cheeks.

Johan was nowhere in sight.

CHAPTER 16
BOREDOM

After five days on the ship, Britta was sick of hunting for Johan. "Mama, I'll watch Arvid, but Johan is old enough to take care of himself. Don't ask me to find him!"

"Now, Britta..."

"Now, Mama!" she snapped. Britta did not mean to be disrespectful; it just seemed to happen. The ship was getting boring, and she had already copied down every English sign posted on the ship. There was nothing to do but walk the decks. "I'll take Arvid with me for a walk around the deck, and if we see Johan, we'll tell him you want him. O.K.?"

Mama lay back on the bottom bunk and sighed.

"Why don't you come along, Mama?"

"No, I think I'll have a rest," she said. It was Mama's third rest that day. Britta hoped she wasn't getting sick. Many of the passengers were coughing and miserable. Maybe she was just sad for Elsa. It was hard to forget her.

Britta took Arvid's thin hand in hers and led him up the sixty stairs to the deck. The third class deck had bolted-down benches, and most of the passengers were up there enjoying the fall sunshine. The air was chilly, and everyone was wrapped in coats and shawls. Britta shivered and reminded herself to dig out more of those warm clothes she had scoffed at a few days ago.

"Can we go up on the nice deck?" Arvid asked her.

"The nice deck?"

"That's where Johan takes me. I'll show you." Arvid led her to a spot where pipes led up to somewhere, and hidden from view beside them was a painted metal ladder. Arvid scrambled up the ladder without a word and motioned Britta to follow. She gathered up her skirts and climbed the ladder to a rooftop, checking first to be sure no one saw her. The roof led to a deserted section of the next deck. Arvid climbed over a railing and waited for her.

"I don't think we should!" Britta whispered.

"Johan said we can," Arvid assured her.

Britta was afraid that people would know they were third class passengers by their clothes, but when they came around the corner onto the main deck, she was amazed to see people dressed much like them in drab homemade dresses and shirts. Of course,

-128-

most of the passengers were well-dressed people with heavy greatcoats and fur wraps, and children in brightly-printed store-bought dresses with ruffles and bows. Adults lounged on wooden deck chairs or strolled along the beautifully scrolled railings looking out over the endless vista of rolling waves.

The vast blue sea. The constant smell of salt. There weren't even any sea birds following them anymore. Britta had lost interest in watching the waves roll against the ship. She missed the meadows and trees and boulders of Finland. She wanted to smell a fresh flower and nibble a handful of tart raspberries. She was tired of the endless rock, rock, rocking of the ship.

Down at the far end of the deck, some older boys were playing a game. They were using long sticks to push flat discs toward a pattern of blue triangles painted on the deck. Britta and Arvid walked over to watch, and who should be playing but Johan!

Johan used his stick to push a disc down to the triangles. His disc cracked against another one, forcing it off the court. His teammates cheered, so Britta and Arvid did, too.

"Hi, Britta. Hi, Arvid." Johan grinned. "Glad you could make it. I'm playing shuffleboard."

Britta smiled. That Johan! She had to admit, this deck was much nicer than theirs, and if she wanted to spend more time up here, she'd better be nice to Johan. She wouldn't say a word about it to Mama.

Britta took Arvid's hand, but he shook her off. "I want to stay with Johan," he said. Britta looked at Johan with a question in her eyes.

"I'll watch him. We'll be back by supper," Johan said.

Britta wasn't sure about leaving Arvid. "Will you be warm enough?"

"Let me be," Arvid shrugged as he stepped over beside Johan. Britta wondered where this attitude had come from– her sweet little brother was becoming another Johan. Heaven forbid!

Johan handed Arvid his game stick and showed him how to hold it. Britta decided that Arvid would be safe with the big boys. If Johan forgot about him (and Britta knew that could happen), Arvid could find his way back; he'd shown her the way there.

A group of girls sat on deck chairs nearby. One wore a crisp navy sailor dress, and the other two wore plaid dresses with starchy bows. As Britta drew closer, she realized they were speaking Swedish! Though they looked a bit younger than her, they might be friendly. They chatted gaily as they played with a lovely porcelain doll, ignoring Britta as she stepped closer. How Elsa would have loved that doll...

Britta closed her eyes to push back the painful memory. Elsa was gone now. As Mama said, "We have to move on."

Britta strolled further along the deck. It was much less crowded than the third-class deck, and she wasn't totally out of place. She heard more Swedish than she'd heard in steerage, and she wondered if she still might find a friend.

She spotted another group of girls who looked more her age. They wore homespun dresses like her, but when she smiled at them, they laughed and turned away. She felt a stab of loneliness and sighed. She didn't recognize their language, anyway. It didn't really matter. She didn't need a friend– she could work on her English.

Further down the deck she spotted something that made her heart skip a beat. There, lying on a deck chair was a large book– Svensk-Engelsk Lexikon (Swedish-English Dictionary). Whose could it be? She yearned to pick it up and look at it. She walked around it, then settled quietly in the chair beside it to wait for its owner to appear. Would it be a grown up? A grandparent? Oh, dear God, please let it be a girl just my age. We could spend the rest of our trip learning English together. We could pretend we were English and have such good times! Maybe she'll even have a kitten....

Britta watched as person after person

came by, waiting to see who would pick up the dictionary. No one came. Maybe someone had lost it. Would it be so terrible if she picked it up to look at it? If a person left it lying around, wasn't it fair to take a peek? She could say she was looking for a name inside the cover so she could return it. She reached a hand to touch its leather binding, then decided not to. Her cheeks burned. She didn't want anyone to think she might steal.

She waited and waited, and as she waited she dreamed of their landing in America. They would show their thirty dollars, and Papa would be waiting there with open arms and a hundred more dollars. He would take them to their beautiful home in Minnesota. He would have a new dress for her and a new hat for Mama and maybe a gun for Johan. He would have toys for Arvid and Elsa.

Goodness– Papa doesn't even know that Elsa died! How terrible! Britta sighed. No wonder Mama was so sad and tired with four of her children already gone. But everything will be better in America, Britta assured herself. And she would speak English. She and Papa. They would teach the rest of the family this new language, and they would all make a new life in America.

A long, lean arm reached for the dictionary. Britta looked up into the face of a young man. A boy, actually, maybe a few years older than she was. He had serious

brown eyes and dark brown hair-lots of it. He was very handsome, Britta thought. Her heart skipped a beat. Should she say anything? Her face flushed.

"*Hello*," she said in English.

"*Hello*," he replied, then picked up the dictionary and walked off.

Britta's heart sank. That was that, then. Just an English hello.

She heaved herself up, stiff from sitting so long. She trudged back along the deck, climbed over the railing and down the ladder, and headed back down to steerage. Nothing was going right today.

Mama and Johan were sitting on the

bottom bunk talking.

"Where's Arvid?" Mama asked.

Johan sneered. "Didn't Mama ask YOU to take care of him?"

"Johan!" Britta scolded, glaring at him.

"Britta, I trusted you to watch your little brother. He's too young to be left alone!" Mama said.

"Johan will help me find him," Britta answered. "Come along, Mr. Man of the Family."

"What if he fell overboard?'" she whispered to Johan as they started toward the stairs. "No one would even know. He's too little to be left alone!"

"Don't worry, Britta. He'll be fine," Johan sneered. "He's not a baby, you know."

Britta wasn't so sure. The boat was a big place for a frail little boy, and Mama even worried about Johan. She knew better than to say it, though. She hurried off ahead, calling "Arvid! Arvid!" up and down the decks. She could have killed Johan right then. Why couldn't he act like the Man of the Family once in a while? What was wrong with him?

"Hey, Britta!" Johan called from behind her. "Look! Here he comes!"

Arvid was skipping down the deck with a huge grin on his face. He ran past both Johan and Britta, and down the stairs to steerage. By the time Johan and Britta caught up, he was nestled in his mother's arms. "I had such FUN, Mama! I'm big enough to take care of myself, see?"

"Well, we'll see about that," Mama said with a laugh as she smoothed his curls and hugged him close.

Johan stuck his tongue out at Britta, then tapped her on the shoulder and took off up the stairs at a run. "I'll get you, Johan!" Britta laughed as she raced after him, her blonde braids flying.

CHAPTER 17
WIND AND WAVES

Britta woke in the night to the stench of vomit, and within minutes the pitching and heaving of the ship started her stomach churning, too. Arvid moaned beside her and she reached over to feel his forehead. It was cool. Thank goodness.

Moans and retching sounds filled the dark room. Britta shuddered at each splatter onto the floor. Now and then it would be a hollow, metallic sound when someone made it to one of the huge spittoons, but not often enough. Britta lay back, eyes open, willing herself not to be sick. Once it started, there would be no stopping.

"I feel sick, Britta," Arvid whispered.

"I know, Arvid. So do I. Just lie back with your knees up and take deep breaths. Try to think of happy things like birch trees and sunshine. It won't be many days now before we'll be running through meadows of grass."

"I'm thinking of Elsa," he whispered.

"Make it a happy thought, Arvid."

"It is. She's smiling."

Britta swallowed hard. Arvid was lucky; her memories of Elsa always brought tears. She forced herself to think of birch trees and buttercups– and Papa.

Somehow, the long night passed. When Johan opened the porthole to clear the air the next morning, a wave washed across him, drenching his quilt. He slammed the porthole and locked it. "Still storming," he announced in a dull voice.

When the kitchen workers finally brought breakfast down to steerage, only a few of the passengers straggled to the tables. Britta pulled on her boots before she stepped onto the open floor. She returned with slices of white, crusty bread for Arvid, Johan, Mama, and herself. "It might help to nibble just a little bit at a time," she said.

"Thank you, Britta," Mama said in a weak voice, though she didn't even reach for the bread. Britta set it beside her on the bed. Johan, Arvid, and Britta sat together on the flat-topped trunk with their backs to the room, trying to ignore the stench and the retching as they took tiny bites of bread. Arvid pinched his nose shut.

"Plug your nose from the inside," Britta suggested. "You can squeeze it from inside and you won't smell anything."

"How?" Arvid asked. "I can't do it, and it

STINKS in here."

"Can we go up on the deck?" Johan asked.

"I think it might be too dangerous," Mama said. "A wave could wash you overboard."

"It won't, Mama. I can hold the railings. I'll be careful," he said as he rose to leave.

"Please don't, Johan..." Mama said.

"Johan?" Britta snapped. "Why don't you think about someone else for a change, instead of just yourself?"

"Like who?" he snapped.

"Like Mama. Did you ever think that maybe she worries about you?"

"I can take care of myself!" he said, storming off.

"Four children gone already. Dear God, protect him..." Mama began. Her tired voice broke off.

Britta knelt by Mama's bunk. "Don't worry. He'll be careful," she said as she brushed a wisp of hair off Mama's forehead. Her skin felt hot. Oh, dear God. Not Mama!

Britta rummaged in the trunk for a rag, went to the water barrel to wet it, then draped it over Mama's forehead. She pulled the quilt from her bed and added it to Mama's covers. What else could she do? They had no medicine. She would have sent Johan for help if he hadn't taken off again. She clenched her fists. He was so selfish!

"I'll be fine, Britta. I just need rest," Mama whispered, patting Britta's hand. "Don't worry."

Johan returned with a scowl. "No one is allowed on deck because of the storm. They have an officer posted at the stairs. We all have to stay down here."

Johan and Arvid climbed up on the top bunk to watch the storm through the port-hole, and Britta decided to join them. There was nothing else to do. Mama needed to sleep. "AAK! Johan! Your quilt is sopping wet!" Britta said, yanking it off the thin mat-tress and heaving it over the side rail to the floor. They would dry it later up on the deck.

Rain pelted the window, and waves like giant hills roared toward them. Each wave crashed against the side, washing the porthole under water for a moment before the ship lurched the other way.

"Whee!" Arvid squealed each time the ship heaved. The excitement of the storm had eased his queasy stomach. Mama lay silent on the lower bunk. Britta hoped she was only seasick. There was nothing more to be done for her until they could reach the ship's doctor. She wished Mama was stronger, but Mama was Mama, after all.

If only Papa were with them, things would be so different. Britta remembered a time when Papa had held her in his lap as a huge storm drove across the meadow at Vistaso. She had jumped at each crack of thunder, but Papa had laughed and tickled her until she was laughing, too. Papa could make this terrible storm fun, too, Britta thought. Soon they would be a family again—in maybe just a week.

The storm settled that afternoon, and a late lunch of mutton soup and biscuits was delivered to steerage. Though many of the passengers couldn't bear to even look at food, the children wolfed down their meal. Britta brought a bowl of soup to Mama, who lay still and silent in her bed. Britta rearranged the quilts to prop Mama's head, then spooned the warm broth for her.

"Johan, will you go find the ship's doctor and ask him to come and see Mama?" Britta said.

"How will I ever find him? And who's going to translate for me?"

"Find someone who speaks Swedish and see if they'll help you," she said. "You're The Man of the Family– remember? So try acting like one!"

It was a long time before Johan returned with news. Britta was sure he'd decided to play with his friends on the upper deck. "The ship's doctor is busy with first class passengers now, then he'll go to the second class, and later tonight or tomorrow he'll be down to check the passengers in steerage." Britta's shoulders slumped, but she rubbed her mother's shoulder. "Don't worry, Mama. We'll take care of you." She lifted the rag from Mama's forehead and went to cool it in the water barrel. She felt Mama's forehead again before replacing the rag. Still hot.

"I'll take Arvid with me while you take care of Mama," Johan announced.

"Thank you so very much, kind brother," Britta said with a sideways glare at Johan. As usual, Johan would be playing while she worked. Well, at least she could study her English words while she sat with Mama. Maybe she could even teach her some English. She hoped Mama hadn't caught pneumonia during those last days at the hospital with Elsa.

"I think I might have caught a fever from the family a few bunks over," Mama said in a strained voice. "I held their sick baby so the mother could tend to her little ones. She was so tired. We speak different languages, but help is the same in any language." Mama smiled weakly.

Why would Mama risk catching a fever like that? Britta couldn't scold her, though. Mama was already being punished for her foolishness.

The doctor didn't get to the steerage deck until the following morning. He spent quite a long time with the sick baby, but he was unable to communicate with the mother. He sent one of her older children to the deck with a note.

Soon a sailor came down to join the doctor, and Britta listened as they spoke in hushed tones. First the doctor spoke in English, then the sailor translated. The mother responded to him, then the sailor translated that back into English for the doctor. Britta understood only a few of the English words, but she could tell by the hushed tone of their voices that it was serious. The doctor opened his bag and gave the baby a shot, but he shook his head sadly and patted the woman's shoulder before he left them.

Britta jumped from the trunk, walked over to the doctor and said in clear English, "*My mother sick.*"

The doctor turned to her and smiled, nodding. "*Where is your mother? What is wrong with her?*"

Britta let him to Mama and said, "*Hot.*"

The doctor felt Mama's forehead and took out a thin, glass tube, which he washed carefully before putting it into Mama's mouth. Britta had no idea what it was. "*What is that?*" she asked.

"*It's a thermometer, to check her temperature.*"

"*Thermometer,*" Britta repeated, trying to remember. She didn't know what it did, but it was bound to help Mama.

"*What are her other symptoms?*" he asked Britta.

She shook her head. She didn't understand. The doctor held Mama's wrist and looked at his watch. Britta had no idea what he was doing, but it might help, too. Anything would help.

The doctor took a small brown bottle out of his bag and poured two drops of its contents into a cup of water. "*Two drops in a cup of water at breakfast, at lunch, at dinner, and before bed. Do you understand?*"

"*Two at breakfast, lunch, dinner, bed,*" Britta responded with a nod. She knew the words breakfast, lunch, dinner, and bed. She would give Mama a cup of water with medicine at each of those times. She beamed at the doctor and said, *"Thank you."*

"You're very welcome, my dear. Your mother will be just fine."

Britta nodded, although she wasn't quite sure what he'd said. It didn't matter–she would give Mama the medicine, and she would soon be well.

After the doctor left, she picked up her pencil stub and wrote three new words in her dictionary: *"thermamter," "tempacher,"* and *"medsin."*

Tomorrow she would find the boy with the Swedish-English dictionary.

CHAPTER 18
THE DICTIONARY

The next morning, Britta's heart lightened when she woke to sunlight glinting through the portholes into steerage. The room still reeked of vomit, but people were opening their portholes to the fresh sea air. A few passengers were methodically mopping the floor—sploosh, swish, swish. It was a soothing sound, and Britta hoped it would help clear the air. As children woke, sounds of chatter began to fill the room. Britta climbed over Arvid to check on Mama, who lay with her eyes open listening to the waking room.

She smiled up at Britta. "I'm feeling better today."

"I'm so glad, Mama." Britta smiled as she walked to the water barrel to fill a cup for her medicine. "*Medsin*," she said aloud. That must mean medicine in English. Now what did "*thermamter*" and "*tempacher*" mean?

After their breakfast of white bread, cheese, and milk, Britta pulled out her dictionary. She ruffled through the five pages of hotel stationery and smiled as she surveyed her work. English words were scrawled in every direction, and many had Swedish translations beside them. The spelling might be wrong, but the words were English!

She tucked the papers into her pocket, grabbed her shawl, and announced, "I'm going up on the deck. Johan, you'll have to watch Arvid and take care of Mama for a while." Johan's mouth was stuffed with bread, so when he tried to stop her, all he could get out was "Muggumffff!" Britta ignored him and kept right on going. She had some rights, too. The Man of the Family could take on a few responsibilities!

A light breeze blew across the deck, and Britta stood a moment at the railing to inhale the fresh salt air. The waves were low rollers that hardly rocked the ship. Sky and water stretched forever. The sky was a brilliant blue, and the ocean was a shade darker. All Britta could see was a vast world of blue, blue, blue.

Very few passengers were up strolling and lounging on the deck. Those who had been sick from the storm were probably still sleeping. Britta loved the quiet of early mornings on the deck, especially after the constant noise and bickering in steerage, which gave her a headache.

Britta quickly found the ladder to the

second-class deck, determined to find her friend with the dictionary. She smiled at the thought. Her friend. She had said one English word to him, and he had answered with the same word. Well, she might be shy about making friends, but this time she had a reason to be friendly. She wanted to see that dictionary! It wasn't really so very selfish, she told herself– English would help her family. It already had. She'd used her English at the dock and again yesterday with the doctor. She was getting better all the time.

Britta checked over her shoulder before she climbed the ladder, and once she got to the roof, she spotted a tall, stiff officer in a black uniform heading her way on the second-class deck. She dropped to the roof and crouched behind a chimney, her heart thumping in her chest. She held her breath and said a quick prayer.

The officer unlocked a gate in the railing and stepped onto the roof. Britta's heart caught in her throat. Had he seen her? He stood by the pipes and chimneys and lit a cigarette. At long last, she heard his footsteps heading back across the roof, then the clink of the gate. His footsteps grew faint. Britta heaved a sigh of relief, looked around one more time, and clambered over the railing onto the second-class deck. She smoothed her skirts and arranged her shawl around her shoulders before starting her hunt.

She passed the same group of girls playing with their dolls and smiled at them. They still ignored her. A few ladies lounged nearby in deck chairs, their legs covered with plaid wool blankets. One of the ladies sniffed pointedly when Britta walked by, but the other one smiled. When I'm rich, Britta thought, I'll be nice to everyone.

There were a few men playing the game with sticks and flat discs, and she stopped to watch for just a minute. It was a complicated game, but they seemed to enjoy it. She walked the deck, checking every chair for the boy with the Svenska-English Dictionary. She couldn't find him anywhere.

She decided to sit in the deck chair where she'd spotted the dictionary a few days before. Maybe he was the kind of person who always sat in the same spot. Britta closed her eyes and basked in the warm sun. Her chair was protected from the breeze, and she was comfortable even without a blanket. When Britta heard the chair creak next to her, she opened her eyes.

It was him!

"*Hello!*" she blurted in English.

He looked over at her, and her breath caught. He was so handsome!

"*Oh. Hello again,*" he said, then turned to his book. It was the dictionary!

"Do you speak Swedish?" Britta asked, this time in Swedish.

"Yes. I'm from Sundsvall, Sweden. And you?"

"I'm a Swede-Finn from Kvevlax, near Vaasa."

"Oh," he said. "That's nice." He bent over his dictionary, a shock of brown hair falling over his forehead and hiding his eyes. He pushed it away from his forehead, then flipped through a few pages in his dictionary. His finger searched down the page, pointing to each entry as he labored over it.

Britta cleared her throat. "Could you help me with something?" she asked. Making friends with him wasn't nearly as easy as it had been with Hilda.

He turned his head to her once again and sighed. "I guess so. What is it?"

Britta pulled her dictionary pages from her apron pocket and unfolded them. She pointed to the words *"thermamter"* and *"tempacher"*. Can you tell me what these words mean?

He took the papers from her and examined them. "What is this mess?" he asked, holding up the crumpled pages with words and notes scrawled every which way in smudgy pencil.

Britta blushed. It wasn't a mess– it was weeks and weeks of hard work! She wanted to snatch the pages from his hands and run away, but she forced herself to stay. She wanted to see his dictionary. She wanted a friend. Britta blinked back a tear.

The boy looked over at her, tilted his head, and smiled. "Oh, I'm sorry! It's just hard to read. That's all. How did you find all these words?"

"We've been living in Liverpool for many weeks, and I've written down every English word I could remember. I work every day to memorize them. A shop woman and a hotel worker helped me, but I found most of the words by listening and by reading signs. My spelling is bad, but I did my best."

"In Sundsvall the girls don't even go to school," he said, looking directly into Britta's eyes. "How much school have you had?" he asked.

She looked straight back into his brown eyes, which was like looking into a deep, dark well. She almost felt dizzy. "I've gone to school every year, but not all the time. My papa's been in America, so I had to work on the farm. I only go to school during the winter, but I work hard and learn fast."

"I see that. Well, I can help you find your words, I guess." He sat forward on his chair and held his dictionary open so she could look at it with him. The printing was very small, and Britta had to bend close

"I wonder if you need glasses," he commented. "Do you always bend so close over your reading?"

Britta blushed again. "I don't know."

"Well, let's see... *'thermamter.'* Do you mean *'thermometer'*? Here it is. It means 'an instrument for measuring temperature or fever.' Does that sound like what you're looking for?"

"I think so. It was a long, glass stick that the doctor put in Mama's mouth." she said.

"Yes, that's it. You can write it on your paper." Britta reached into her pocket and realized she hadn't grabbed her pencil stub.

"You can use my pencil." His sharp pencil made a clear, clean mark on the paper, and Britta could squeeze the Swedish translation in a much smaller space than usual.

"Now how about *'tempacher'*?" she asked.

"Temp... How about *'temperature*: a measurement of heat in an object or in the air.' Does that sound right?"

"Yes. Like a fever, right?" Britta labored to correct her spelling of 'temperature' and add the Swedish word for 'fever.'

"Well, it's more than just a fever, I think. It sounds like it's a word that means the temperature of anything, like the air or a kettle of water," the boy explained.

Britta added a few more words to her definition. *"Thank you,"* she said, returning his pencil.

"Would you like to know any other words? I'm learning, too, you know." The boy smiled at her for the first time. He had straight, white teeth that gleamed in the sunlight.

"Oh, yes! Please!" Britta said, beaming. Her new friend helped Britta look up the English words she hadn't been able to translate into Swedish: bank, captain, passengers, theatre, dining, station, pier, customs, and many, many more. The morning sped by as they struggled to figure out the correct spelling for each of the words, but the boy had a good sense for English sounds, and they found nearly every one.

By the time they had finished, Britta's dictionary was a tangle of cross-outs and scribbled definitions. She finally stood up, clutching the pages to her chest. "Oh, thank you! By the way, what's your name?" she asked.

"Hans Erik," he replied. "What is yours?"

"It's Britta. Britta Jacobson," she said, smiling. "I'll see you later!" she said as she skipped gleefully back to tell Mama.

"Hans Erik," she repeated to herself. "Hans Erik."

CHAPTER 19
DANCING

Mama was sitting at the table sipping tea when Britta returned to steerage. She looked up and smiled as Britta took a seat across from her.

Johan scowled. "Did you have to be gone all morning?"

"Yes, I did," she said. "And guess what, Mama? I've made a new friend who has a Swedish-English dictionary, and we looked up all the words I didn't know. Look!" Britta laid her dictionary pages on the table, grinning.

"So what?" Johan said, his eyes narrowed into angry slits. "She's probably another blabbermouth like Hilda."

Britta rolled her eyes but didn't say a word. What Johan didn't know wouldn't hurt him. Anyway, he'd probably tease her.

Shipmates in white uniforms clattered down the stairs with kettles of stew for their noonday meal. They wiped their hands on their aprons, which were already a work of art in brown, red, and yellow stains. Another sailor carried a huge bag of white bread on his back, while others brought a vat of milk and a barrel of pickled herring. Britta took her bowl and cup to stand in line with the others. She wondered what Hans Erik would be having for lunch. Would his lunch be served on china, or were the second-class meals like theirs? She wondered if he had to face herring at every meal– dried herring, smoked herring, baked herring, and fried herring. Britta would be glad if she never saw another herring in her life.

When she got back to the table, Johan was wolfing down his stew as Mama looked on with a smile. "It's been a long morning for Johan, Britta. He hates it down here."

"Well, it doesn't hurt him to help out once in a while," Britta mumbled. " Johan hadn't even thought about food for Mama. How like him. "Here," she said, setting her bread and stew in front of her mother. "I'll go get another bowl."

"Thank you, Britta. I think I feel up to eating today."

The line had grown, and as Britta took her place at the end, a mournful wail cut through the room, sending shivers up her spine. She remembered hearing her mother cry like that after Elsa died, and she searched the room for the source of the death moan. It was the mother Mama had helped with the sick baby. She sat rocking her baby, her gaping mouth open in an agonized cry. The woman's two other children stood at their mother's side looking bewildered and helpless.

Britta left her place in line and touched the shoulder of the mother, who hardly noticed. Then she took the hands of the children and led them over to sit at the table with Mama and Arvid. Johan was gone. She broke a slice of bread in two and handed half to each of them. The children stuffed them into their mouths, never taking their dark eyes off their mother. Britta wondered if they'd had breakfast. She went back to the line and got them each a bowl of stew and a cup of milk, which they gobbled hungrily as they watched their mother rock her dead baby.

Mama sat up with tears streaming down her cheeks. "I must go to her. I can't talk with her, but pain can be shared without words."

"But Mama! That's where you got your fever!" Britta argued.

"That poor woman shouldn't be alone!" Mama's voice was stern as she stood to join the woman.

Britta sighed. Mama was right. She had helped the children, hadn't she? And she'd done it without a thought. She turned her attention back to them. They were about two and three, both with thick brown hair and full, round cheeks. They looked like little chipmunks. Arvid looked big next to them, though he was still thin and pale. His skin looked ghost-like next to their brown cheeks and dark eyes.

"You finish your lunch, Arvid. We need to get you healthy, too!" she ordered.

There was a small burial service for the baby on the steerage deck that evening. Mama and Britta stood near the melancholy woman and her children as the captain, dressed in a sparkling white uniform, said a few words in English. Britta tried to follow what he said, but she could only understand a word here and there. She had a lot of work to do if she was going to finish learning English in just one more week.

The baby's body was laid in a tiny box with flowers spread over it. The captain said some words to the mother, then made a sign of the cross over the baby. Another woman sang a song in a beautiful clear voice. Britta recognized the tune, but the English words were strange to her. It was lovely, though, and it gave her goose bumps. She wished someone had sung for Elsa. Had that only been a week ago?

But nothing prepared Britta for what came next.

Two sailors in clean uniforms stepped forward and picked up the tiny coffin. They stepped to the railing and dropped it over the side into the swirling, rolling sea. Britta was horrified. How could they? She ran to the rail to see it bob in the waves for a while, then disappear beneath the water. The flowers floated on the surface, a momentary reminder that a child's life had been lost at sea. The baby's mother crumpled onto the deck, sobbing uncontrollably.

"Oh, Mama!" Britta whispered as she ran back into her mother's arms. They stood together on the deck, reliving their own pain over their lost Elsa– sweet little Elsa.

They stood quietly on the deck for a long while as the crowd dispersed. Someone brought the woman and her children back down to their bunks, and soon people were strolling around the deck as though nothing had happened.

As they walked along the deck to the steerage stairway, lively violin music wafted from the other end of the deck. Britta took Mama's hand and followed the music, which brought back vivid memories of Papa. "Oh, Mama, it's just like Papa playing. And we can hear his violin in just one week. I can't wait!"

A crowd had gathered around a gray-haired man in a tattered brown coat who stood on a box playing his fiddle. A younger man played a tall, skinny drum, and someone else banged two wooden blocks together in rhythm. A dark-haired woman stepped back from the crowd and broke into a dance, her arms waving and her legs kicking furiously. Her red printed skirt twirled as she danced, and long, dark curls escaped from her scarf and flew around her head. Britta marveled at her hoop earrings– she had pierced ears like a pirate! Soon more dancers joined her, and the air was filled with music, laughter, and clapping.

Was it all right to be happy after a funeral? Britta turned to ask Mama, but she was already clapping and nodding with the music, her eyes glowing. Britta grinned and joined in. The musicians and dancers lifted their spirits as the sun painted the sky pink, then lavender.

Britta had never been up on the deck in the evening– had they danced every night? She studied the feet of the dancers, trying to match their movements in her mind, then with her feet, but with tiny, little steps. If she could learn English, she could certainly learn to dance.

"Britta! Mama!" a voice called from behind them. "Isn't this great?" Johan said. "There's a dance every night. Watch!" He joined the group of dancers, kicking out his heels, first one, then the other. Britta laughed at how silly he looked, but he was having such fun! She yearned to join in, but she was not quite ready. She picked out a tall red-haired woman in an embroidered shawl who she thought was the best dancer of all. Britta copied her movements with tiny steps as she clapped and laughed with the crowd.

Mama tapped Britta's shoulder and spoke loudly into her ear. "Arvid is tired. I'm taking him down to bed. You can stay here with Johan, but be sure to stay together."

Britta grinned. "Thank you, Mama. Good night."

She turned back to the music, clapping and stepping to the beat as Johan cavorted among the dancers. Before long someone hung a kerosene lantern from a hook on the mast, and the shadows of night grew darker and deeper around the bright circle of activity. The lantern shone on the dancers' faces, glistening with sweat. Everyone was caught in the frenzy of activity, and Britta's heart thumped as wildly as if she were out there with them.

When she stepped outside the circle of light, she was amazed at the brilliant canopy of stars above her. She had never seen so many at one time. At home in Finland, the stars shone directly above their house, but here the stars totally surrounded her. Stars shone above the ship and around it, even reflecting from the water. Britta felt lightheaded and a bit dizzy, floating on this sea of stars.

"Hello, Britta."

Britta turned, her eyes wide. "Hello,

Hans Erik."

"Isn't this fun? I come down to this deck to watch them dance every night. There's no dancing in second class except for formal dancing inside."

"You just watch? Why don't you join them?" Britta asked.

"I don't know. I guess I'm a little shy about dancing. I don't know how."

"I feel the same way. I'd love to try, but I'm afraid to do it wrong."

"Oh, I don't think there's a wrong way–look at that funny boy with the white hair, just kicking his legs and twirling around. It doesn't look much like dancing, but he's having a great time."

Britta giggled. "That's my brother."

"Oh. I'm sorry," Hans Erik said.

"Maybe that's why we just want to watch," Britta said, smiling up at Hans Erik. They stood side by side watching the dancers, clapping and tapping to the beat of the music. Britta's sad feelings were washed away by the music. And by Hans Erik.

After a long while, Johan stepped up to Britta.

"Are you ready to go down?" Johan asked between heaving breaths.

"I guess so. Are you done dancing?" If he could call it dancing.

"I'm worn out. And I'm thirsty, too. Let's go," he said as he headed off. Britta waved a silent goodbye to Hans Erik, then followed Johan along the deck.

"Did you like it?" he asked as they headed toward the stairs.

"I loved it!"

"Then why didn't you dance?" he asked.

"I don't know, Britta said. "Maybe next time."

"You're silly," Johan said.

"So are you!" Britta laughed.

When they got down to their bunks, Mama hushed them. "Arvid's not feeling well," she said. "I think he has a fever."

"Oh, no!" Britta cried. "Why can't things ever go right? I wish Papa were here!"

CHAPTER 20
STORM BREWING

Britta dreamed that night of dancing with Hans Erik. He held her in his arms and twirled her around the deck, their laughter filling the air. When she opened her eyes, though, her first thought was Arvid.

She leaned over her bunk railing. "How is he, Mama?"

"I think he's better. His fever is less, and he sipped some water during the night," Mama whispered.

"Maybe he has what you had, Mama. Should we give him some of the medicine from the doctor?"

"I used the last few drops yesterday. Could you go find the doctor and ask for more? Do you think he'd come down to see Arvid?"

"I'll go see, Mama." Britta hopped down from her bunk and deftly pulled her dress on under her night shift, then pulled her night shift off over her head. She chuckled at how skilled she had gotten at dressing without undressing. Living in a huge room with a hundred other people meant little privacy. Some of the people chose to wear their clothes day and night, but Mama insisted that her children wear nightclothes to bed.

Britta grabbed a piece of bread from the breakfast table before hurrying to the deck to ask for the doctor. Once again, she wished Papa were here, but he wasn't. They had to take care of things themselves. Britta was glad she had worked so hard to learn English. It was helping them over and over.

She spotted a man in uniform walking the deck and stepped in front of him.

"*You speak Swedish?*" she asked in English.

"*No. I speak English,*" he answered.

"*Where is...doctor?*" Britta asked.

"*Second class deck, I believe,*" he said. "*What's the problem?*"

"*Brother... sick ... and ... fever.*" Britta screwed up her face as though she were going to cry– that would show him how serious it was.

"*I'll take you up there, luv.*"

He led her up the ladder she already knew well, unlocked the gate, and held it open for Britta to come through. She pretended that she'd never seen the second-class deck, stopping to stare wide-eyed at the wooden deck chairs and the plumed bonnets of the ladies.

"Nice, eh?" the officer said.

Britta wasn't sure what he'd said, so she nodded. *"Thank you,"* she said with a smile. Her mind was busy sorting out the English words she would need to talk to the doctor as she followed the sailor to the entrance of a huge, beautiful room. Light streamed in through tall stained glass windows, and gas lights on the walls added to the brightness. People sat at separate tables with with white linens, and waiters carried huge trays of food to each table. Britta gasped.

The officer told her to wait at the door, then went to stand silently at the doctor's table as he finished his meal. Someone tapped on her shoulder. *"Good morning,"* a gentle voice whispered in English. It was Hans Erik!

"Hello, Hans Erik," she answered, her cheeks crimson. He continued through the doorway to sit at a table with an elegant looking man and woman. His parents, Britta thought. They must be very rich.

She was startled to see the doctor standing before her. *"And how can I help you, little miss?"* he said kindly.

Britta wasn't sure what he'd said, but she launched into her explanation. *"Brother sick fever you come medsin?"*

The doctor put his hands up in the air and said, *"Slow down, Missy. Let's have it again."* Britta blushed. She didn't understand

-164-

his words, but his hands told her to slow down.

Britta took a deep breath. "*My brother ... sick ... fever. You come? Medsin?*"

The doctor looked at his watch and said, "*I'll be down later, but here's some of the drops now if you think it will help.*" He reached into his bag and pulled out another small brown bottle and handed it to her.

"*Give him one drop in a cup of water at breakfast, one drop in a cup at lunch, one at supper, and one at bedtime. Do you understand?*"

Britta nodded. Just like with Mama, she thought. "*Thank you, Doctor,*" she said with a nod. Before leaving, she glanced over at Hans Erik, who didn't look up. Her mouth watered at his plate heaped with eggs and biscuits and ham. She wanted to talk to him, but not here. Maybe later...

As the officer walked her back to the gate, he looked up at the sky and commented, "*Looks like a nasty storm comin'. Best bunker down.*"

Britta recognized the word "*storm*" and followed his gaze. Huge, dark clouds were piling ahead of the ship. Though the sun was still shining behind them, the ship was heading into something ominous. As the officer let her through the gate, she waved goodbye.

"*Thank you!*"

"*Happy to help you, luv.*"

By the time she got back to steerage, Johan was already gone, and Arvid was sitting up sipping some tea. Britta handed Mama the pills.

"Have you eaten yet, Mama? You should see the dining room in second class. They eat at separate tables– eggs and biscuits and ham and fruit. It's wonderful, Mama!"

"Well, we're in third class, Britta, and lucky that we're on the ship at all. Eat your bread and cheese and be thankful."

Britta scowled and decided not to mention that a storm was coming. Mama might make her stay below, and she wanted to go back to the second class deck to find Hans Erik. Her stomach fluttered as she thought of him, and her cheeks felt hot. Could Mama tell?

"I'm going back up on the deck, Mama, to keep watch for the doctor. He said he'd come down when he could."

Britta stuffed her dictionary pages into her pocket and headed up the stairs. She glanced at the darkening sky as she walked to the ladder. She checked both ways and nearly flew up the ladder, across the roof, and over the railing. Whew!

She went straight to the deck chair where she'd met Hans Erik, and there he was, sitting with a blanket over his legs, reading his *Svensk-Engelsk Lexikon*.

"*Hello, Hans Erik,*" she said as she

perched on the open chair beside him.

He smiled at her warmly. *"Good morning, Britta."*

"I'd like to learn some more English words," she said. "I've brought my dictionary pages, and I can make more room...I think."

"There's a part in the front of the dictionary about grammar. Would you like me to teach you some verbs and some connecting words?"

"Oh, yes!" Britta said.

"And I have something for you," he said, turning to the back of his dictionary. He pulled out a clean sheet of white paper and handed it to Britta. "It's from our room. For letters, I expect, but you'll put it to better use."

"Oh, thank you!" Britta exclaimed.

"Now a very useful English word is *"the"*, which you put in front of words that are things..." he began as Britta wrote *t-h-e* on her new dictionary sheet.

Time sped by as Hans Erik taught Britta from the front of his dictionary. She repeated each new word and entered it onto her new page as neatly as she could. She didn't notice the clouds rolling heavier and darker toward the ship. She didn't notice the sun disappear. She didn't notice the passengers looking at the sky and commenting. She didn't notice that there were fewer and fewer people on the deck. She didn't notice anything but Hans Erik, until...

"Britta's got a boyfriend! Britta's got a boyfriend!" Johan and two of his friends jeered.

"He's not a boyfriend! He's my FRIEND!" Britta said, her cheeks burning. Leave it to Johan to ruin her lessons!

"Sure. A boy and a girl sitting together with their heads together is just FRIENDS! I don't think so!" a red-headed boy taunted.

Britta lifted up her dictionary sheets. "See? We're learning English, and this is proof! So there!"

Johan grabbed the sheets and looked at them with a sneer. "Looks like just a lot of scribbling to me! Probably love notes!" he yelled. The boys broke into raucous laughter. Britta looked to Hans Erik. Why didn't he do anything? He just sat there with his book on his lap, staring at the boys.

A tall, dark-haired boy grabbed the papers out of Johan's hands to look at them. "Love notes! Love notes!" he yelled, then held them out over the railing. Britta was aghast. She jumped up to grab them back from him. Johan looked at her, at Hans Erik, and at the papers.

"Give them back to her," Johan said. "It really is her dictionary."

Britta couldn't believe it– the boy was going to throw them overboard, and Johan was taking her side!

Just then a violent burst of wind whipped across the deck. It ripped the papers from the boy's hand and scattered them overboard. Britta watched horrified as they tumbled and fluttered over the waves. Each one settled on the water, floated for a moment and was gone.

Britta turned on her brother. "That was my dictionary! Weeks and weeks and weeks of work! It's all your fault, Johan! All my English! Gone! And it's all your fault! I hate you! I hate you!" She threw herself at Johan, pounding at his chest, her fury unleashed. All her frustration from waiting in Liverpool and her pain from losing Elsa and her fears for Arvid– she pounded it all out on Johan's chest.

A crack of thunder shook the ship, and the other boys scattered. Britta and Johan were the only ones left on the deck.

"Stop it, Britta! Stop it! You're crazy! It's only some stupid papers!" he yelled. Lightning flashed across the sky, and thunder cracked.

"A storm is coming! We have to go in!" Johan gripped her wrists and dragged her along the deck toward the ladder.

"Let me go!" Britta screamed, twisting away from his grasp. "Leave me alone!" she shrieked as she raced down the deck away from Johan.

CHAPTER 21
THE STORM

The wind slapped Britta's braids across her cheeks as she ran, and it tore at her skirt and shawl. Deck chairs blew over and clattered against the deck, straining against the ropes that kept them from washing overboard. Britta heard a booming announcement repeated over and over in different languages: "*Passengers go directly to your cabins.*"

Britta didn't care. She just wanted to run– run away from everything and everyone. Her cheeks burned and tears of anger stung her eyes. She slipped on the deck and grabbed the railing to break her fall. The wind was fierce! What could she do? She'd have to go in, but there was no doorway nearby. She clung to the railing, pulling herself along, hand over hand. When she came to the triangle game painted on the deck, she spotted a narrow closet just tall enough for her to squeeze into. She pushed the game sticks aside and pulled the door tight. Once safe in the darkness, she buried her face in her hands and sobbed. She heard Johan calling for her. "Britta! Britta!" She didn't care. She didn't want anybody.

Soon the ship was pitching violently. Britta's stomach lurched. She knew she should go below. Mama was probably worrying about her. She wondered what Johan would tell Mama. She opened the door and peeked out. There was no one in sight. The sky was dark, the wind was wild, and the deck was pitching back and forth. Did she dare? She decided to run for it. As she raced past the tumbling deck chairs, the ship lurched and she lost her footing. She was thrown down onto the deck, and an excruciating pain jolted through her ribs. She curled up in agony, then felt herself slipping sideways– toward the sea!

"Help!" she shrieked, flailing to grab something– anything to keep her from sliding overboard! Just as her legs slid over the edge toward the water, she caught the railing with her right arm. Lightning shocked the deck to brightness for only a second, followed by a deafening crack of thunder. Britta clung with all her strength and dragged her legs back onto the deck, grimacing at the pain in her right side. The ship pitched back the other way, slamming her body against the deck again. The ship tossed her around like a rag doll. The wind pounded against her, and then the rain came. Sheets of it drove at her face,

her arms, her hair, like knives slashing at her skin.

"Oh, Dear God. Help me!" she screamed as she clung desperately to the railing.

The ship pitched violently the other way, and Britta wrapped both arms around the railing. She was alone. She would have to save herself.

She knew she could never make it back to steerage. Mama would be worried, but she couldn't think about that right now. She'd have to find a safe place to ride out the storm. She looked across the deck at the closet where she'd hid, but there was no way she could get herself back there with nothing to hold onto. Oh, why had she ever left it?

She squinted ahead, straining to see through the pelting rain. She spotted a length of rope snaking from an open hatch about ten feet ahead of her. As the ship continued pitching and heaving, she reached her right arm ahead on the railing and wrapped it around the rail before she released the grip of her left arm. That way she was able to inch forward. It was slow progress, and pain stabbed at her side each time she moved. Whenever she planted her feet on the deck, a wave would sweep them out from under her. Inch by inch she progressed toward the rope, unsure even what it was attached to. What if it was just a loose rope? Would she be swept overboard? She wouldn't think about that now. She had to have faith in God– and in herself. Somehow she wasn't panicking. In her whole life she had never been in so much danger, yet her mind was clear.

When she finally got to the rope, she decided to test it before she let go of the railing. With her right arm wrapped securely around a rail, she reached as far as she could with her left arm. The rope looped just out of her reach. Did she dare let go for just a second? Not for a rope that might not be attached to the ship! Not with this pitching and lurching. Without the railing she would be overboard in an instant. No America and no Papa. She had to think!

She waited for the ship to pitch toward

the water again, then with both arms wrapped around a post, she reached toward the rope with her foot. Whoosh! A wave crashed across her and swept her body away from the rope.

Britta closed her eyes, said a quick prayer, and waited again for the boat to pitch toward the water. When she looked up, another big wave was rolling toward her. She closed her eyes, ducked her head, and held fast. When she looked again, she saw that this wave had washed the rope closer!

The third time the boat pitched toward the water, Britta reached out with her foot, hooked the rope, and pulled it beneath her. She wrapped both feet around it so it would not get washed away by the next wave, then paused to catch her breath. With the wind and waves buffeting her, she reached down with her left hand and grasped the rope, which was so fat she couldn't even get her hand around it. She yanked at it, and it held at the other end. Thank God! It was secured inside the hatch.

She managed to loop the rope around her left leg as she clung to it with her left hand, but she couldn't make herself let go of the railing. Her right hand clung desperately to the railing. She knew she could trust the railing, but could she trust the rope? It still might break loose. The wind and rain lashed at her face. A colossal wave nearly tore her from the railing. She had to get inside!

Britta waited for the ship to pitch up away from the water, then dove to the deck, grabbing at the rope with her right hand and wincing at the pain in her side. She snaked her way along the rope, keeping it wrapped around her legs as she worked first one hand, then the other along the rope. It took forever, with the ship pitching back and forth and the waves crashing over her. Finally she reached the trap door. The compartment below her was totally dark, but she had no choice. She twisted her body around to lower herself feet first as she clung to the rope with one hand and the hatchway door with the other. Her feet touched something– floor?– before her head was even down inside the hatch.

Britta thought it must be a rope storage, because all she could find when she groped around was rope and rope and more rope. She was lucky that the hatch had fallen open and a rope had broken free. She braced herself inside a huge coil of rope, then dragged her own rope in so she could close the hatch. She felt a piercing pain in her side with each pull. At least the waves weren't pounding at her any more.

Once Britta had all the rope inside, she reached up to pull the hatch down over the opening. That was when she started to shake. All the fear she had pushed out of her mind now heaped on her tenfold. She might have died out there! She could have been swept overboard and drowned! And all because she was mad at Johan. Britta couldn't believe her stupidity. She repeated the ordeal over and over in her mind as tears streamed down her already-wet cheeks. Her stomach tensed and shivered until she vomited. At long last, totally spent, she collapsed in the coil of rope. Britta slept through the rest of the storm.

When she woke, the ship was rolling gently. She pushed herself up and reached above her. She could see slivers of light around the hatch, and she felt for a handle or latch. There was nothing! She was trapped!

Britta pounded on the hatch. "Help!" she called. "Let me out!" There was no answer, so she kept pounding. Before long she heard a reassuring voice from the other side. It wasn't long before it was followed by a scraping sound against the hatch, and it was lifted.

A face with an officer's cap peered down at her. *"And how did you get in here, miss?"* he asked with a grin. *"You look a bit wet."*

Britta squinted out at him. *"Swedish,"* she said, then *"Thank You"* in English. The man took her arm and lifted her gently through the hatchway. She winced as he pulled at her right arm.

A group had gathered to watch the officer help her from her prison. Britta was sure they thought her foolish to hide during the storm. She blushed, straightened her back and smoothed the wrinkles in her sopping wet dress. She forced a smile, then turned to find her way back to steerage.

As she headed down the deck, she saw Johan walking toward her. "Britta!" he cried when he saw her. "I thought you'd gone overboard! Mama has been frantic." Then he added, "I'm so sorry. I hunted for you as long as I could, but the ship's officers made me go in."

Britta walked right past Johan as though she hadn't seen him.

When she got down into steerage, Mama cried, "Thank God you're alive!" then folded her arms around her so tightly Britta winced.

"Ouch, Mama! my ribs! I took a bad fall and I think I hurt myself. It hurts a lot."

Mama rummaged through the trunk for Britta's other dress. Once Britta had pulled her wet things off, Mama wrapped her in a quilt and rubbed her hard to stop her shivering.

"Wherever have you been, Britta? I was sure I'd lost you!"

"Oh, Mama. I'm so sorry. So sorry. I was so foolish." Still wrapped in the quilt, Britta told Mama all about her meetings with Hans Erik and her English lessons and how Johan's friend had tossed her dictionary papers into the sea. She told about being stuck on the deck in the storm and finding her way into the rope hatch. She didn't tell her how bad the storm was on the deck or that she might have died. Mama didn't need to know those things.

"Oh, Mama. I lost my shawl, too. I'm so sorry! It must have blown overboard."

"Better a lost shawl than a lost daughter," Mama said. "What can I say, except that I'm glad you're alive– and I love you very, very much."

Once again, mother and daughter stood in each other's arms, tears streaming down their faces.

"Mama?" a little voice piped from the bunk.

"Oh, Arvid! What is it?" Mama asked gently, turning to him.

"I don't feel good, Mama. I think I'm going to throw up," he said. Mama held a bucket next to him and supported his head.

As Britta looked on, she thought about the strength it had taken Mama to face crisis after crisis. Mama might be quiet, but she handled whatever came her way.

CHAPTER 22
AMERICA!

Arvid lay in bed for two days, unable to keep food down. The doctor shook his head. *"Just keep giving him water. That should hold him until we get to America. It will only be a few days more."*

"Mama," Britta said. "You need some fresh air. Go up on the deck and sit for a while. I'll stay with Arvid."

Johan stayed behind with Britta as Mama gathered her knitting and left. Britta wondered why he hadn't dashed off as he did every morning.

"Britta. I want to talk with you," he said. "You haven't said a word to me since the storm, and we should make up before we get to America."

"Why?"

"Finally, you talked to me!" he said. "One word, but you talked to me." He sat on the trunk and shifted uncertainly. "I'm sorry for what I said, and I'm sorry Jorgen dropped your dictionary papers. It was my fault– I knew they weren't love letters."

"So you're sorry. I could have died out there in that storm, and you say you're sorry."

"I tried to find you, Britta– I really did, but the officers made me go in. When I thought you might have drowned, I felt like drowning myself, too."

Britta thought a moment. She had heard him calling, and it had been her own stubbornness that kept her out in the storm, not Johan. "All right, I'll accept your apology. But I'll never forget what a cruel thing you did."

Johan hung his head. "Do you want me to watch Arvid so you can go out?" he offered. "Thanks, but I told Mama I'd watch him, and I remember the last time you said you'd watch him." Johan blushed. "Maybe you could go sit with Mama for a while. Entertain her with stories about your adventures on the ship or something."

"That wouldn't entertain her," he grinned. "It would make her furious. I'll go sit with her, though," he said, pulling on his red shirt. He smiled at Britta as he left– actually smiled.

Britta marveled at the change in her brother, The Man of the Family. She wondered if maybe he had grown up on this trip. She knew she had. When Papa left, she had thought the world would end, but it didn't. They had managed without him, though life wasn't quite so fun as it might have been. Mama had gotten them to the train and the ships, and Britta and Johan had managed through the long, hot, painful summer in Liverpool. Papa would be astonished at how much they had changed in four years. Would he even recognize them?

Oh, Papa! She'd hardly had time to think of him lately, and they would see him in just a few days. She hoped he was still in New York after all these months. Was he still meeting every ship? Did he know they were on this one? Mama hadn't had the money to send a telegram. What if he wasn't there?

Britta said out loud, "We will face what comes."

"What, Britta?" Arvid asked.

"Oh, nothing. Just something Mama says. Do you want to learn something really important in English? Say this: '*I love you, Papa.*'"

"*I love you, Papa.*"

For the next few days, Britta sat with Arvid in the mornings, teaching him English words when he was awake. He grew paler and thinner each day, but he was still smiling–and alive. Britta wondered if he was pining away for his twin, but she never mentioned Elsa. No sense in making things harder for him.

Britta spent her afternoons with Hans Erik working on English. "I've brought you more paper, Britta. You can start a new dictionary," he'd said the first afternoon after the storm.

"No thank you, Hans Erik. I don't want to start all over again. I've decided I can learn English in my head."

Hans Erik gazed straight into her eyes and nodded. "You have a strong spirit, Britta."

Britta blushed. "It's time to get busy," she said, turning to the next page in the dictionary.

The last few evenings Britta and Johan went up on the deck for the dancing, which was always lively and fun. Britta eventually joined in, and found she could lose herself dancing. Though Hans Erik never joined in, he was always there, smiling and clapping along. Britta and Johan would come back down to steerage flushed and excited, then collapse into a sound sleep.

On the twelfth day, Britta and Hans Erik were studying as usual. A small boat pulled up alongside the ship, and a man in a pilot's cap climbed aboard. He spoke English, and Britta was thrilled that she could understand most of what he said to the people who met him on deck. *"I'm here to pilot the ship into the New York Harbor. Tomorrow you'll see land, and that land will be America."*

The passengers cheered, and many of the men threw their hats into the air. One cap floated over the railing and into the ocean. Everyone laughed except the man who stood capless with a startled expression on his face. Then he, too, burst into a hearty guffaw. Everyone's spirits were high, but none could be higher than Britta's– she was sure of it.

"We'll be there tomorrow!" she said to Hans Erik as they returned to their deck chairs. "Tomorrow I'll see my Papa for the first time in four years!"

"Four years?" he said. "I can't believe you've been without a father for four years. You never told me that!"

"You never asked," Britta said, her eyes gleaming with excitement. "All we ever talk about is English. I can't study any more right now. I have to tell Mama!" she said, then skipped down the deck. "See you later!" she called over her shoulder.

Because the pilot had made his announcement on the second-class deck, the people in steerage hadn't heard. "Mama! We're going to land in America tomorrow! We're nearly there!" Britta called across the huge room. The passengers who understood her Swedish clapped and cheered. Soon the whole room was buzzing with excitement. Though they might not understand the details, they all knew the word "America."

Mama and Britta danced a jig together next to their bunks, and Arvid climbed out of bed to join them. Britta marveled at the energy he mustered to celebrate the news. His little feet were skipping faster than either hers or Mama's. Johan came racing down to tell them the news, and his furrowed brows showed his disappointment when he saw that they already knew. His disappointment was short lived, though, as he was caught up in the excitement of the room. Soon violins and harmonicas were playing, and everyone was dancing– in the middle of the afternoon!

That night no one slept. The air was filled with excited sighs and whispers and the sounds of people tossing and turning in their bunks.

Britta lay in her bunk dreaming of Papa and their new home. She couldn't wait to tell him how much she'd missed him– in English! She couldn't wait to see his sparkling green eyes. She couldn't wait to throw her arms around his neck. She imagined a tall, white house with green shutters and lacy curtains at the windows, just like one she'd seen on a picture postcard. She thought about the gifts Papa would have for each of them. She wanted a store-bought dress– a bright flowered dress with a big yellow bow at the back. She wondered if she'd see Hilda in Minnesota. Lisel must be a grown cat by now, maybe with her own brood of kittens! Oh, there would be so much to see and do in America. She could not wait for tomorrow!

As the first streaks of dawn lit the

room, Britta bounded from her bunk. "Let's go up and try to see America!"

Johan rubbed the sleep from his eyes, peered through the porthole, then hopped down to join her. "Do you want to come, Mama?" she asked.

"I'll stay here and let Arvid sleep. I'll see America soon enough," she said. By the time they got up on the deck, it was crowded with passengers eager for their first view of their new country. Johan led Britta to a ladder she hadn't noticed before, and they climbed it to see above the crowd. As the sun rose behind them, they spotted a thin, dark line across the horizon ahead.

"That's it!" someone cried. "That's America!" The crowd exploded in a cheer. "America! America!" people cried. Tears streamed down Britta's cheeks as she joined the cheer for that tiny strip of land that was to be their new home. "Oh, Papa!" she cried, "we're coming!"

She looked up to smile at Johan, but he was no longer above her on the ladder. She saw a boot disappear over the railing high above.

"Oh, Johan!" she said, shaking her head.

Later that morning, Britta slipped up to say goodbye to Hans Erik. He was sitting in his usual spot poring over the dictionary. "Last minute lessons," he said with a laugh.

"Are you excited?"

"Excited?" Britta exclaimed. "I'm almost bursting. I can't bear to wait another minute! Let's look!" She and Hans Erik joined the passengers at the railing to watch the land mass grow larger as the ship approached. In second class the deck was less crowded than in steerage. Britta didn't think these people were quite as excited, either.

"*Thank you for helping with English me, Hans Erik,*" Britta said with a pleased smile. "*I learn a lot with you.*"

"*You are welcome,*" he replied.

"I must go now to help Mama pack. Maybe I'll see you again some time," she said, sorry to say goodbye to this boy who she'd dreamed might be more than a friend.

"Wait," he said. "I have something for you." Hans Erik handed her the dictionary.

"Oh, no, Hans Erik. I can't take this."

"You must," he said. "I can buy a new one in New York, and they may not have them in Minnesota." He winked. "You never know!"

Britta hugged the dictionary to her chest. "Oh, thank you, Hans Erik. Thank you!" and without a thought, she gave him a quick kiss on the cheek.

Britta nearly flew back to steerage, where she showed Mama the dictionary. Inside the cover she found the message:

"To Britta. All my best from your good friend Hans Erik Nilson, *The Baltic*, August,

1904.

"It's my first book, Mama. My first book for our new life in America!"

"One of many firsts, I'm sure," Mama said with a smile.

"But now I need your help to pack our things."

CHAPTER 23
ARRIVING

"Mama," Britta said as they folded the quilts, "I heard someone say in English that the best dressed passengers would be the first to leave."

"Well, we don't have much, but we'll wear our best then," Mama said.

They pulled out their brightest shawls, and Britta was thankful that Mama had insisted on washing their clothes during the voyage, even though they'd only had salt water. Britta brushed her long hair until it shone, and Mama braided it in tight, neat braids, tied with the blue ribbon that had been Lisel's leash. Britta wondered where Hilda might be now. She'd already been in Minnesota for three whole months.

Britta scrubbed Arvid's face and hands as Mama did up her own hair, and they both checked to make sure they had gotten everything packed.

"There is plenty of room left in the trunks. Do you want to pack that heavy dictionary?" Mama asked.

"No, I'll carry it," Britta said hugging it to her chest. "I can study while we wait."

"I expected that," Mama said with a smile. "Where's Johan? I haven't seen him all day!"

"He'll be back, Mama. We can just leave his good clothes out on the trunk lid. If I know Johan, he'll probably just get back in time for landing. Let's go watch up on the deck."

Mama held Arvid's hand as the ship glided into a channel. "Look at the mountains!" Arvid piped.

Britta could feel the excitement in his voice, and peered through the pink-tinted haze to where he was pointing. She grinned. "Those aren't mountains, Arvid. They're tall, tall buildings. I think they must be the tallest buildings in the whole world."

"Wow," Arvid answered. "And is Papa there?"

"I'm sure he is, and he's been waiting a long time for us."

Britta noticed more and more boats around them. Tugboats and other boats of all shapes and sizes filled the narrowing river. They spoke to one another with whistles and toots, and every once in a while *The Baltic* would answer with its own deep, echoing voice. Everyone on the deck talked excitedly in a hundred different languages, and children asked question after question.

"Mama! Britta! Arvid!" Johan appeared beside them in his good clothes, grinning from ear to ear. "We're here! Isn't this fine!"

"And finally, you're with us, too. Please stay with us now, Johan," Mama said.

"Yes, Mama. But do you know where I've been? I've been on the top deck where the captain steers the boat, and I've seen the Statue of Liberty already. We'll be coming by it before long, I think, and on this side of the ship, too."

"I want to see! I want to see!" Arvid crowed.

Britta could see there was no hope of pushing to the railing, but she had an idea. "How about climbing on Johan's shoulders, Arvid? Is that all right, Johan?"

"Sure," he agreed, lifting his feather-light brother up over his head. "Gosh, he doesn't weigh anything!"

"I can see! I can see it!" Arvid cried, pointing ahead. Britta was surprised that he even knew what he was talking about. In seconds, though, she saw the huge form of the Statue of Liberty looming just ahead of the ship.

The crowd grew silent as they passed the statue. Hans Erik had told Britta that this gift from French schoolchildren was a symbol of America's welcome to people from all nations. Tears filled her eyes as she looked up at the torch welcoming them to America– their

new home.

And the next welcome would come from Papa! Britta's heart nearly leapt from her chest.

Many of the passengers had already brought their trunks up to the deck, so Johan and Britta headed down to lug theirs up, too. "Let's carry them together, one trunk at a time," Britta suggested.

"Can't handle one alone?" Johan taunted. Britta almost kicked him, but thought the better of it. She shook her head, smiled, and took one handle of the round-topped trunk. It took all their strength combined to manage the six flights of steps. They were both out of breath by the time they reached the deck.

"Let's go get the other one, quick, Britta, so we don't miss anything."

"I'll beat you down!" Britta said as she skipped away. Britta was ahead on the stairs, laughing as she dodged passengers on the way. On the last flight, Johan took a flying leap from midway down and landed ahead of Britta.

"Looks like I beat you, little sister," he grinned.

"Looks like you did," she answered with a grin. Nothing could spoil this day for her— not even Johan. They grabbed the handles of the other trunk and began their last ascent up the steerage steps.

Before long, the ship's officers had sorted the emigrants and their belongings into groups on the deck. Once the ship had been guided to a pier, the passengers with steamer trunks were the first to board the barge to Ellis Island. Johan and Britta struggled to drag their trunks down the steep ramp onto the ferry called the *General Putnam*.

Britta glanced up to the second class deck to see if she might spot Hans Erik, but he wasn't there. Then she realized that the upper class passengers were getting off directly onto the pier on the other side of the ship. Didn't they have to go to Ellis Island, too? She was confused and a little angry. Was America going to be a country where money was all that mattered?

Well, she'd be rich very soon. Maybe in just a few minutes.

Hundreds of passengers huddled on the deck of the barge with their luggage. Wind whipped across the harbor, tugging at their shawls, bonnets, and scarves, but nothing could dampen Britta's spirits. She looked ahead at the red brick buildings and turrets that towered over the tiny Ellis Island, wondering if Papa would be at the dock waiting for them. Oh, she hoped he would! To pass the time, she read the words in the front of her dictionary. "To Britta. All my best from your good friend Hans Erik Nilson, *The Baltic*, August, 1904." It wasn't just an impulsive last-minute gift. Hans Erik had PLANNED to give it to her. Life just couldn't be better!

CHAPTER 24
ELLIS ISLAND

Papa wasn't standing at the dock when they landed. No one met the barge except men in blue uniforms, who warned the passengers to watch their luggage carefully because there were thieves around. The emigrants dragged their luggage across a courtyard and up a wide staircase. Britta and Johan left one trunk at the bottom with Mama and Arvid while they dragged the heavier one to the top. Britta waited at the top of the stairs to guard the first trunk while Johan went back down to Mama. She helped him drag the lighter one. Arvid tried to help, too, but he barely had the strength to climb the stairs.

They stepped into line to get through customs, and Britta realized it was another medical check. How could they refuse to let people in after their long voyage? If someone was sick, they needed to see a doctor, not go back to Liverpool! Britta saw another little boy as thin and pale as Arvid at the front of the line. A man in a black uniform wrote something on his back with white chalk, and his family wasn't allowed through. They were sent to another line. Though she didn't know what it meant, she decided that she wouldn't let anyone mark Arvid. Maybe her English would help.

The medical check was horrible. A man flipped back Britta's eyelids with a funny metal hook, and they poked and prodded and questioned her. They talked so fast she could not understand anything they said, then they pushed her through. She waited as Johan was passed through, then they both watched carefully as Mama and Arvid were investigated. When the medical officer pointed to Arvid and asked Mama questions, Britta pushed her way back through the line, smiled at the medical officer and said, "*Seasick. Very seasick. Not sick.*"

The medical examiner nodded to Britta and passed Arvid through without a mark.

They dragged their trunks to the next room, a huge, high-ceilinged room that was even bigger than the train station in Liverpool. Britta and Johan stopped wide-eyed at the entrance, but Mama shuffled them along. "Don't stand in the doorway. Let's find a line."

"But which is the right line, Mama?" Britta asked. The room was divided into sections, with metal cages and lines of wooden benches between them. She had no idea where to go.

"Read the signs, Britta. You can figure it out."

"Ireland, Norway, Sweden, Finland ... That's it over there, Mama. Finland!" Britta turned to help Johan with the trunk, but he was gone. "Oh, no! Mama? Where's Johan?"

They surveyed the area nearest them, but there was no sign of Johan. "We'd better wait," Mama said. "He'll be back. Maybe he had to use the toilet."

"He could have told us! Sometimes he just doesn't think." Britta wanted to get in the line. It was just like Johan to hold things up, and Papa was probably waiting on the other side!

"*Move along. Move along. Find the right line and line up!*"

"They said we have to go, Mama. We have to find our line. We'll go to the Finland line. Johan can find us there, and we can save his place in line. Look at all the people coming behind us." There was a huge mass of emigrants streaming into the big room. Britta was astonished to see dark-skinned people in colorful draped robes and small Chinese men with thin braids down their backs. There were men with flat black caps and little braids down the sides of their cheeks. What odd things other people do, she thought. She wondered if they found her odd, too, with her long blonde braids and her bright blue shawl.

"Arvid, you help me drag the heavy trunk and Mama can get the other one," Britta ordered. Arvid beamed up at her as he pulled at the leather handle. His end barely budged, but he kept straining at it as Britta pushed it toward the Finland line. Mama followed them dragging the lighter trunk, and they all kept watch for Johan. Britta couldn't imagine where he had gone.

They waited what seemed like hours in the noisy, crowded room. When they got near the front of the line, Johan still hadn't turned up. "Wait here, Mama. I'll see if I can find him."

Britta found an officer standing near the door and asked in English, "*Have you seen the brother? He is tall, blonde hair, and Swede-Finn. He is lost.*"

"*I don't know that I have, Miss. Let's check the lost people room.*" He led Britta to a small room filled with crying children and forlorn-looking adults. Johan wasn't there. Britta shook her head. "*No brother here.*"

The officer thought. "*If you are a Swede-Finn, does that mean you speak Swedish?*"

"*Yes, Swedish,*" Britta answered.

"*Then take a look at the Sweden line. Maybe he's over there. He might have looked for people who speak his language.*"

Britta headed over to the "*Sweden*" sign, and sure enough, there was Johan standing alone near the end of the line, his eyes red and puffy.

"Johan!" Britta cried.

"Britta! Britta! Thank God I've found you!" he said, running to her. He even gave her a hug.

Britta grinned and shook her head. "You found ME? Oh, Johan. Why did you ever leave us? What happened?"

"I thought I saw Papa through that gate over there," he said pointing, "and I ran over to talk to him through the wire. It wasn't Papa after all, and I got caught in a mob of people, and when I couldn't find you, I got scared I might never get through. I have no money, Britta, and I don't have my passport. They wouldn't let me through without them. I know it!"

"But why did you go in the Sweden line?" she said as they began weaving their way through the crowd back to Mama and Arvid.

"I didn't know it was the Sweden line. I kept asking people for help, but no one understood me. Finally one of the officers led me to this line. I was hoping you'd be waiting for me at the other side and hand me my passport and money so I could come through. Oh, Britta, I'm so glad to see you!"

"And I never thought I'd say it, Johan, but I'm glad to see you, too! Now let's get back to the right line and get through to find Papa."

"Johan!" Mama scolded. "You are sure to be the death of me. My family is nearly together now. Only one more set of questions, I hope," Mama said. "You hold the thirty dollars, Johan, and you take our passports, Britta. You can answer the questions."

After an endless set of questions, the immigration officer checked to be sure they had enough money, wrote in their passports, entered their names on a register, then passed them through.

The small family dragged their trunks through the doorway, squinting at the bright sunlight of the open courtyard. Britta scanned the expectant faces of the crowd outside, searching for Papa. She heard Mama shriek, "Johan Erik!" and run into the arms of a man much shorter than Britta remembered. Mama sobbed as she clung to him, a flood of emotions that brought tears to Britta's eyes, too. When Mama finally stepped back to wipe her tears and straighten her hair, Britta recognized Papa's wavy, blonde hair, his green sparkling eyes, and his soft, reddish beard. He extended strong, welcoming arms to his children, and Britta flew into his embrace before he could even say her name. *"We're here, Papa! We're home!"* she cried.

After crushing her in a giant bear hug, he held her by the shoulders and shook his head, grinning. "My goodness! A fine looking young flicka you've grown to, Britta. And you speak English! You make me proud." Britta's heart soared. She didn't need any gifts. All she wanted was her Papa. And to be a family again.

"And this must be Johan!" Papa said, extending his hand to Johan, then pulling him into a hug with his other arm. Johan stood stiff in his papa's embrace, fighting a private battle with tears. "A fine, young man! So tall and strong!" Johan beamed.

Arvid stepped up to Papa with a question in his eyes. "And could this be Arvid?" Papa said, bending to lift him. "So thin and pale!"

"*I love you Papa.*" Arvid said, in nearly perfect English.

"*And I love you too, little man.*" Papa smiled. He set Arvid down on the trunk, then leaned over to whisper to Mama. "He's so thin! He'll never live long enough to become an American." Though she wasn't meant to hear, Britta was aghast. What if Arvid heard that?

"He's strong, Johan Erik. Strong like all of us," Mama replied, her loving gaze resting proudly on her three children.

"And where's little Elsa?" he asked.

Mama shook her head. Tears filled her eyes. "She wasn't quite so strong, Johan Erik. Elsa is with God."

Britta felt a stinging in her throat– that old feeling she had swallowed back time and time again. Tears brimmed in her eyes, too, as she remembered Elsa, that bright little sprite of a sister who had shared her kitten in secret. Poor, poor Elsa.

Papa's green eyes iced over, and his mouth grew tight. After a long silence, he said, "I never should have left you. It was too much. And to make the voyage alone. I'm so sorry.... I never thought it would be so long.... So many years.... So many months for you to cross."

Mama reached to his shoulder. "But we're here now, Johan Erik," she said with conviction. She wiped the tears from her cheeks and continued. "It is time to leave the tears behind and look ahead. We're a family again, ready for our new life."

Mama was right, Britta thought. It was time to move on. Elsa was with God. Britta looked at her family with new eyes.

Arvid had been sick, but he had survived. He was thin, yes, but he would grow stronger. Papa would see.

And Johan– Johan wasn't really so bad. He would love America, and wouldn't have to be The Man of the Family any more. He'd be free to seek all the new adventures he could find. And he certainly would!

And Mama. Britta saw Mama in a new light– strong in her own quiet way. She had led her family through four years in Finland and all the way to America. Mama was a survivor, and now she could relax and let Papa be in charge.

Britta was eager for her new life in America. She would work hard on her English, and she could teach the others. Maybe Papa would help her.

Papa opened his arms once more, welcoming his entire family into his embrace. The crowd around them melted into a blur as they stood together in the warmth of his love. "We'll never be separated again," he promised. "We are a family now and for always."

A horn tooted from the waiting ferry. "Time to be on our way!" Papa announced as he released them and reached for one of the trunks. "Time to introduce you to New York!"

Britta's heart soared as she joined Johan to drag the other trunk, eager for their new life– with Papa.

EPILOGUE

Britta and her family settled on the North Shore in Minnesota, where they faced many more adventures. Although Papa thought Arvid would never live to become an American citizen, he grew to be a strong, healthy man. In fact, everyone in the family became citizens, and all three children lived full, happy lives. Britta lived to be 78, Arvid lived to be 80, and Johan lived 89 years. Four more children were born to Maria and Johan Erik on their homestead in northern Minnesota.

Every family has a story– whether it seems exciting or not– filled with both struggles and joys. Whether your ancestors crossed an ocean or a continent to settle in a new place or whether they've always lived in the same area, it's likely that their lives were very different from yours. Take the time to talk to your older relations about their memories, their childhoods, their parents and their grandparents. It's because of a family history gathered and written by Eleanor Jacobson Stone that Britta's story could be written for you.

ABOUT THE AUTHOR

Ann Marie Mershon is an English teacher and outdoor lover who teaches, writes, hikes, skis, bikes, canoes, and kayaks around her wilderness home near Grand Marais, Minnesota. She enjoyed many hours talking with Eleanor Stone about her family's emigration.

ABOUT THE ILLUSTRATOR

Gail Alden-Hedstrom is an artist who expresses herself through many different mediums– from batik to beadwork, paint to pencil. She lives on Devil Track Lake near Grand Marais, Minnesota, and is happiest working in her Babes in the Woods studio.